A CLASSI
OUT

M000190661

Trainor's Tower. It was an unbelievable sight—a gigantic two-and-a-half mile high building with one of world's finest astronomical observatories found at the very top. But what else was up there, and what all could be seen from such a lofty, prestigious spot? These were the burning questions that reporter William Windsor wanted the answers to. With access to the tower he believed he could tell the "Tale of the Century." Soon Windsor was given his greatest wish, and upon looking out through that massive telescope, his life—and the lives of many others—would never be the same again!

The late Jack Williamson's writing is nothing new to science fiction fans. He is heralded as one of the great authors of the Golden Age of Science Fiction Literature. "The Prince of Space" is certainly one of his best early tales.

FOR A COMPLETE SECOND NOVEL, TURN TO PAGE 103

CAST OF CHARACTERS

WILLIAM WINDSOR
Historian, observer, writer, reporter, detailer. He was a conscientious witness to mankind's survival.

DR. TRAINOR
An obscure college professor laughed at because of his ambitious plans—but who was laughing now?

MR. CAIN
He was dubbed "The Mysterious Mr. Cain." No one seemed to know much about him, but that was about to change.

CAPTAIN BRAND
A Security Official sent out to find, retrieve and deliver the notorious Prince of Space—a road he'd traveled before.

CAPTAIN SMITH
Loyal servant of the Prince of Space, he was determined to do whatever his Commander—and Earth—needed him to do.

PAULA TRAINOR
The doctor's beautiful and highly desirable daughter, she had eyes for only one man. Would she get her guy, or die trying?

THE PRINCE OF SPACE

By
JACK WILLIAMSON

ARMCHAIR FICTION
PO Box 4369, Medford, Oregon   97501-0168

*For more information about Armchair Books and products, visit our
website at…*

www.armchairfiction.com

Or email us at…

armchairfiction@yahoo.com

CHAPTER ONE
Ten Million Eagles Reward!

"Space Flier Found Drifting with Two Hundred Dead!
Notorious Interplanetary Pirate—Prince of Space—Believed
to Have Committed Ghastly Outrage!"

Mr. William Windsor, a hard-headed, grim-visaged newspaperman of forty, stood nonchalantly on the moving walk that swept him briskly down Fifth Avenue. He smiled with pardonable pride as he listened to the raucous magnetic speakers shouting out the phrases that drew excited mobs to the robot vending machines, which sold the yet damp news strips of printed shorthand. Bill had written the account of the outrage; he had risked his life in a mad flight upon a hurtling sunship to get his concise story to New York in time to beat his competitors. Discovering the inmost details of whatever was puzzling or important or exciting in this day of 2131, regardless of risk to life or limb, and elucidating those details to the ten million avid readers of the great daily newspaper, *The Herald-Sun,* was the prime passion of Bill's life.

Incidentally, the reader might be warned at this point that Bill is not, properly speaking, a character in this narrative; he is only an observer. The real hero is that amazing person who has chosen to call himself "The Prince of Space." This history is drawn from Bill's diary, which he kept conscientiously, expecting to write a book of the great adventure.

Bill stepped off the moving sidewalk by the corner vending machine, dropped a coin in the slot, and received a copy of the damp shorthand strip delivered fresh from the presses by magnetic tube. He read his story, standing in a busy street that rustled quietly with the whir of moving walks and the barely audible drone of the thousands of electrically driven heliocars, which spun smoothly along on rubber-tired wheels, or easily lifted themselves to skimming flight upon whirling helicopters.

Heliographic advices from the Moon Patrol flier *Avenger* state that the sunship *Helicon* was found today, at 16:19, Universal Time, drifting two thousand miles off the lunar lane. The locks were open, air had escaped, all on board were frozen and dead. Casualties include Captain Stormburg, the crew of 71 officers and men, and 132 passengers, of whom 41 were women. The *Helicon* was bound to Los Angeles from the lunarium health resorts at Tycho on the Moon. It is stated that the bodies were barbarously torn and mutilated, as if the most frightful excesses had been perpetrated upon them. The cargo of the sunship had been looted. The most serious loss is some thousands of tubes of the new radioactive metal, vitalium, said to have been worth nearly a million eagles.

A crew was put aboard the *Helicon* from the *Avenger*, her valves were closed, and she will be brought under her own motor tubes to the interplanetary base at Miami, Florida, where a more complete official examination will be made. No attempt has been made to identify the bodies of the dead. The passenger list is printed below.

Military officials are inclined to place blame for the outrage upon the notorious interplanetary outlaw, who calls himself "The Prince of Space." On several occasions the "Prince" has robbed sunships of cargoes of vitalium, though he has never before committed so atrocious a deed as the murder of scores of innocent passengers. It is stated that the engraved calling card, which the "Prince" is said always to present to the captain of a captured sunship, was not found on the wreck.

Further details will be given the public as soon as it is possible to obtain them.

The rewards offered for the "Prince of Space," taken dead or alive, have been materially increased since the outrage. The total offered by the International Confederation, Interplanetary Transport Lunar Mining Corporation, Sunship Corporation, Vitalium Power Company, and various other societies, corporations, newspapers, and individuals, is now ten million eagles.

"Ten million eagles!" Bill exclaimed. "That would mean a private heliocar, and a long, long vacation in the South Seas!"

He snorted, folded up the little sheet and thrust it into his green silk tunic, as he sprang nimbly upon the moving sidewalk.

"What chance have I to see the Prince of Space?"

About him, the slender spires of widely spaced buildings rose two hundred stories into a blue sky free from dust or smoke. The white sun glinted upon thousands of darting heliocars, driven by silent electricity. He threw back his head, gazed longingly up at an amazing structure that rose beside him—at a building that was the architectural wonder of the twenty-second century.

Begun in 2125, Trainor's Tower had been finished hardly a year. A slender white finger of aluminum and steel alloy, it rose twelve thousand feet above the canyons of the metropolis. Architects had laughed, six years ago, when Dr. Trainor, who had been an obscure western college professor, had returned from a vacation trip to the moon and announced his plans for a tower high enough to carry an astronomical observatory giving mountain conditions. A building five times as high as any in existence! It was folly, they said. And certain skeptics inquired how an impecunious professor would get funds to put it up. The world had been mildly astonished when the work began. It was astounded when it was known that the slender tower had safely reached its full height of nearly two and a half miles. A beautiful thing it was, in its slim strength—girder-work of glistening white metal near the ground, and but a slender white cylinder for the upper thousands of feet of its amazing height.

The world developed a hungry curiosity about the persons who had the privilege of ascending in a swift elevator to the queer, many-storied cylindrical building atop the astounding tower. Bill had spent many hours in the little waiting room before the locked door of the elevator shaft—bribes to the guard had been a heavy drain upon a generous expense account. But not even bribery had won him into the sacred elevator.

He had given his paper something, however, of the persons who passed sometimes through the waiting room. There was Dr. Trainor, of course, a mild, bald man, with kindly blue eyes and a slow, patient smile. And Paula, his vivaciously beautiful daughter, a slim, small girl, with amazingly expressive eyes. She had been with her father on the voyage to the moon. Scores of others had passed through; they ranged from janitors and caretakers to some of the world's most distinguished astronomers and solar engineers—but they were uniformly reticent about what went on in Trainor's Tower.

And there was Mr. Cain—"The mysterious Mr. Cain," as Bill had termed him. He had seen him twice, a slender man, tall and wiry, lean of face, with dark, quizzical eyes. The reporter had been able to learn nothing about him—and what Bill could not unearth was a very deep secret. It seemed that sometimes Cain was about Trainor's Tower and that more often he was not. It was rumored that he had advanced funds for building it and for carrying on the astronomical research for which it was evidently intended.

Impelled by habit, Bill sprang off the moving walk as he glided past Trainor's Tower. He was standing, watching the impassive guard, when a man came past into the street. The man was Mr. Cain, with a slight smile upon the thin, dark face that was handsome in a stem, masculine sort of way. Bill started, pricked up his ears, so to speak, and resolved not to let this mysterious young man out of sight until he knew something about him.

To Bill's vast astonishment, Mr. Cain advanced toward him, with a quick, decisive step, and a speculative gleam lurking humorously in his dark eyes. He spoke without preamble.

"I believe you are Mr. William Windsor, a leading representative of the *Herald-Sun.*"

"True. And you are Mr. Cain—the mysterious Mr. Cain!"

The tall young man smiled pleasantly.

"Yes. In fact, I think the 'mysterious' is due to you. But Mr. Windsor—"

"Just call me Bill."

"—I believe that you are desirous of admission to the Tower."

"I've done my best to get in."

"I am going to offer you the facts you want about it, provided you will publish them only with my permission."

"Thanks!" Bill agreed. "You can trust me."

"I have a reason. Trainor's Tower was built for a purpose. That purpose is going to require some publicity very shortly. You are better able to supply that publicity than any other man in the world."

"I can do it—provided—"

"I am sure that our cause is one that will enlist your enthusiastic support. You will be asked to do nothing dishonorable."

Mr. Cain took a thin white card from his pocket, scrawled rapidly upon it, and handed it to Bill, who read the words, "Admit bearer. Cain."

"Present that at the elevator, at eight tonight. Ask to be taken to Dr. Trainor."

Mr. Cain walked rapidly away, with his lithe, springy step, leaving Bill standing, looking at the card, rather astounded.

At eight that night, a surprised guard let Bill into the waiting room. The elevator attendant looked at the card.

"Yes. Dr. Trainor is up in the observatory."

The car shot up, carrying Bill on the longest vertical trip on earth. It was minutes before the lights on the many floors of the cylindrical building atop the tower were flashing past them. The elevator stopped. The door swung open, and Bill stepped out beneath the crystal dome of an astronomical observatory.

He was on the very top of Trainor's Tower.

The hot stars shone, hard and clear, through a metal-ribbed dome of polished vitrolite. Through the lower panels of the transparent wall, Bill could see the city spread below him—a mosaic of fine points of light, scattered with the colored winking eyes of electric signs; it was so far below that it seemed a city in miniature.

Slanting through the crystal dome was the huge black barrel of a telescope, with ponderous equatorial mounting. Electric motors whirred silently in its mechanism, and little lights winked about it. A man was seated at the eyepiece—he was Dr. Trainor, Bill saw—he was dwarfed by the huge size of the instrument.

There was no other person in the room, no other instrument of importance. The massive bulk of the telescope dominated it.

Trainor rose and came to meet Bill. A friendly smile spread over his placid face.

Blue eyes twinkled with mild kindliness. The subdued light in the room glistened on the bald dome of his head.

"Mr. Windsor, of the *Herald-Sun,* I suppose?" Bill nodded, and produced a notebook. "I am very glad you came. I have something interesting to show you. Something on the planet Mars."

"What—"

"No. No questions, please. They can wait until you see Mr. Cain again."

Reluctantly, Bill closed his notebook. Trainor seated himself at the telescope, and Bill waited while he peered into the tube, and pressed buttons and moved bright levers. Motors whirred, and the great barrel swung about.

"Now look," Trainor commanded.

Bill took the seat, and peered into the eyepiece. He saw a little circle of a curious luminous blue-blackness, with a smaller disk of light hanging in it, slightly swaying. The disk was an ocherous red, with darker splotches and brilliantly white polar markings.

"That is Mars—as the ordinary astronomer sees it," Trainor said. "Now I will change eyepieces, and you will see it as no man has ever seen it except through this telescope."

Rapidly he adjusted the great instrument, and Bill looked again.

The red disk had expanded enormously, with great increase of detail. It had become a huge red globe, with low mountains and irregularities of surface plainly visible. The prismatic polar caps stood out with glaring whiteness. Dark, green-gray patches, splotched burned orange deserts, and thin, green-black lines—the controversial "canals" of Mars—ran straight across the planet, from white caps toward the darker equatorial zone, intersecting at little round greenish dots.

"Look carefully," Trainor said. "What do you see in the edge of the upper right quadrant, near the center of the disk and just above the equator?"

Bill peered, saw a tiny round dot of blue—it was very small, but sharply edged, perfectly round, bright against the dull red of the planet.

"I see a little blue spot."

"I'm afraid you see the death-sentence of humanity..."

Ordinarily Bill might have snorted—newspapermen are apt to become exceedingly skeptical. But there was something in the gravity of Trainor's words, and in the strangeness of what he had seen through the giant telescope in the tower observatory that made him pause.

"There's been a lot of fiction," Bill finally remarked, "in the last couple of hundred years. Wells' old book, 'The War of the Worlds,' for example. General theory seems to be that the Martians are drying up and want to steal water. But I never really—"

"I don't know what the motive may be," Trainor said. "But we know that Mars has intelligent life—the canals are proof of that. And we have excellent reason to believe that that life knows of us, and intends us no good. You remember the Enbers Expedition?"

"Yes. In 2099. Enbers was a fool who thought that if a sunship could go to the moon, it might go to Mars just as well. He must have been struck by meteorites."

"There is no reason why Enbers might not have reached Mars in 2100," said Trainor. "The heliographic dispatches continued until he was well over half way. There was no trouble then. We have very good reason to think that he landed, that his return was prevented by intelligent beings on Mars. We know that they are using what they learned from his captured sunship to launch an interplanetary expedition of their own."

"And that blue spot has something to do with it?"

"We think so. But I have authority to tell you nothing more. As the situation advances, we will have need for newspaper publicity. We want you to take charge of that. Mr. Cain, of course, is in supreme charge. You will remember your word to await his permission to publish anything."

Trainor turned again to the telescope.

With a little clatter, the elevator stopped again at the entrance door of the observatory. A slender girl ran from it across to the man at the telescope.

"My daughter Paula, Mr. Windsor," said Trainor.

Paula Trainor was an exquisite being. Her large eyes glowed with a peculiar shade of changing brown. Black hair was shingled close to her shapely head. Her face was small, elfinly beautiful, the skin almost transparent. But it was the eyes that were remarkable. In their lustrous depths sparkled mingled essence of childish innocence, intuitive, age-old wisdom, and quick intelligence—intellect that was not coldly reasonable, but effervescent, flashing to instinctively correct conclusions. It was an oddly baffling face, revealing only the mood of the moment. One could not look at it and say that its owner was good or bad, indulgent or stern, gentle or hard. It could be, if she willed, the perfect mirror of the moment's thought—but the deep stream of her character flowed unrevealed behind it.

Bill looked at her keenly, noted all that, engraved the girl in the notebook of his memory. But in her he saw only an interesting feature story.

"Dad's been telling you about the threatened invasion from Mars, eh?" she inquired in a low, husky voice, liquid and delicious. "The most thrilling thing, isn't it? Aren't we lucky to know about it, and to be in the fight against it!—instead of going on like all the rest of the world, not dreaming there is danger?"

Bill agreed with her.

"Think of it. We may even go to Mars, to fight 'em on their own ground!"

"Remember, Paula," Trainor cautioned. "Don't tell Mr. Windsor too much."

"All right, Dad."

Again the little clatter of the elevator. Mr. Cain had come into the observatory, a tall, slender young man, with a quizzical smile, and eyes dark and almost as enigmatic as Paula's.

Bill, watching the vivacious girl, saw her smile at Cain. He saw her quick flush, her unconscious tremor. He guessed that she had some deep feeling for the man. But he seemed unaware of it. He merely nodded to the girl, glanced at Dr. Trainor, and spoke briskly to Bill.

"Excuse me, Mr. Win—er, Bill, but I wish to see Dr. Trainor alone. We will communicate with you when it seems necessary. In the meanwhile, I trust you to forget what you have seen here tonight, and what the Doctor has told you. Good evening."

Bill, of necessity, stepped upon the elevator. Five minutes later he left Trainor's Tower. Glancing up from the vividly bright, bustling street, with its moving ways and darting heliocars, he instinctively expected to see the starry heavens that had been in view from the observatory.

But a heavy cloud, like a canopy of yellow silk in the light that shone upon it from the city, hung a mile above. The upper thousands of feet of the slender tower were out of sight above the clouds.

After breakfast next morning Bill bought a shorthand news strip from a robot purveyor. In amazement and some consternation he read:

Prince of Space Raids Trainor's Tower

Last night, hidden by the clouds that hung above the city, the daring interplanetary outlaw, the self-styled Prince of Space, suspected of the Helicon outrage, raided Trainor's Tower. Dr. Trainor, his daughter Paula, and a certain Mr. Cain are thought to have been abducted, since they are reported to be missing this morning.

It is thought that the raiding ship drew herself against the Tower, and used her repulsion rays to cut through the walls. Openings sufficiently large to admit the body of a man were found this morning in the metal outer wall, it is said.

There can be no doubt that the raider was the "Prince of Space" since a card engraved with that title was left upon a table. This is the first time the pirate has been known to make a raid on the surface of the earth—or so near it as the top of Trainor's Tower.

Considerable alarm is being felt as a result of this and the Helicon outrage of yesterday. Stimulated by the reward of ten million eagles, energetic efforts will be made on the part of the Moon Patrol to run down this notorious character.

CHAPTER TWO
Bloodhounds of Space

Two days later Bill jumped from a landing heliocar, presented his credentials as special correspondent, and was admitted to the Lakehurst base of the Moon Patrol. Nine slender sunships lay at the side of the wide, high-fenced field, just in front of their sheds. In the brilliant morning sunlight they scintillated like nine huge octagonal ingots of polished silver.

These war-fliers of the Moon Patrol were eight-sided, about twenty feet in diameter and a hundred long. Built of steel and the new aluminum bronzes, with broad vision panels of heavy vitrolite, each carried sixteen huge positive ray tubes. These mammoth vacuum tubes, operated at enormous voltages from vitalium batteries, were little different in principle from the "canal ray" apparatus of some centuries before. Their "positive rays," or streams of atoms, which had lost one or more electrons, served to drive the sunship by reaction—by the well-known principle of the rocket motor.

And the sixteen tubes mounted in twin rings about each vessel served equally well as weapons. When focused on a point, the impact-pressure of their rays equaled that of the projectile from an ancient cannon. Metal in the positive ray is heated to fusion, living matter carbonized and burned away. And the positive charge carried by the ray is sufficient to electrocute any living being in contact with it.

This Moon Patrol fleet of nine sunships was setting out in pursuit of the Prince of Space, the interplanetary buccaneer who had abducted Paula Trainor and her father, and the enigmatic Mr. Cain. Bill was going aboard as special correspondent for the *Herald-Sun*.

On the night before the *Helicon,* the sunship, which had been attacked in space, had been docked at Miami by the rescue crew put aboard from the *Avenger.* The world had been thrown into a frenzy by the report of the men who had examined the two hundred dead on board.

"Blood sucked from *Helicon* victims!" the loud speakers were croaking. "Mystery of lost sunship upsets world! Medical examination of the two hundred corpses found on the wrecked space flier show that the blood had been drawn from the bodies, apparently through curious circular wounds about the throat and trunk. Every victim bore scores of these inexplicable scars. Medical men will not attempt to explain how the wounds might have been made.

"In a more superstitious age, it might be feared that the Prince of Space is not man at all, but a weird vampire out of the void. And, in fact, it has been seriously suggested that, since the wounds observed could have been made by no animal known on earth, the fiend may be a different form of life, from another planet."

Bill found Captain Brand, leader of the expedition, just going on board the slender, silver *Fury*, flagship of the fleet of nine war-fliers. He had sailed before with this bluff, hard-fighting guardsman of the space lanes; he was given a hearty welcome.

"Hunting down the Prince is a good-sized undertaking, from all appearances," Bill observed.

"Rather," big, red-faced Captain Brand agreed. "We have been after him seven or eight times in the past few years—but I think his ship has never been seen. He must have captured a dozen commercial sunships."

"You know, I rather admire the Prince—" Bill said, "or did until that *Helicon* affair. But the way those passengers were treated is simply unspeakable. Blood sucked out!"

"It is hard to believe that the Prince is responsible for that. He has never needlessly murdered anyone before—for all the supplies and money and millions worth of vitalium he has taken. And he has always left his engraved card—except on the *Helicon*.

"But anyhow, we blow him to eternity on sight!"

The air-lock was open before them, and they walked through, and made their way along the ladder (now horizontal, since the ship lay on her side) to the bridge in the bow. Bill looked alertly around the odd little room, with its vitrolite dome and glistening instruments, while Captain Brand flashed signals to the rest of the fleet for sealing the locks and tuning the motor ray generators.

A red rocket flared from the *Fury*. White lances of flame darted from the downturned vacuum tubes. As one, the nine ships lifted themselves from the level field. Deliberately they upturned from horizontal to vertical positions. Upward they flashed through the air, with slender white rays of light shooting back from the eight rear tubes of each.

Bill, standing beneath the crystal dome, felt the turning of the ship. He felt the pressure of his feet against the floor, caused by acceleration, and sat down in a convenient padded chair. He watched the earth become a great bowl, with sapphire sea on the one hand and green-brown land and diminishing, smokeless city on the other. He watched the hazy blue sky become deepest azure, then black, with a million still stars bursting out in pure colors of yellow and red and blue. He looked down again, and saw the earth become convex, an enormous bright globe, mistily visible through haze or air and cloud.

Swiftly the globe drew away. And a tiny ball of silver, half black, half rimmed with blinding flame, sharply marked with innumerable round craters, swam into view beyond the misty edge of the globe—it was the moon.

Beyond them flamed the sun—a ball of blinding light, winged with a crimson sheet of fire—hurling quivering lances of white heat through the vitrolite panels. Blinding it was to look upon it, unless one wore heavily tinted goggles.

Before them hung the abysmal blackness of space, with the canopy of cold hard stars blazing as tiny scintillant points of light, at an infinite distance away. The Galaxy was a broad belt of silvery radiance about them, set with ten thousand many-colored jewels of fire. Somewhere in the vastness of that void they sought a daring man, who laughed at society and called himself the Prince of Space.

The nine ships spread out, a thousand miles apart. Flickering heliographs—swinging mirrors that reflected the light of the sun—kept them in communication with bluff Captain Brand, while many men at telescopes scanned the black, star-studded sweep of space for the pirate of the void.

Days went by, measured only by chronometer, for the winged, white sun burned ceaselessly. The earth had shrunk to a little ball of luminous green, bright on the sunward side, splotched with the dazzling white of cloud patches and polar caps.

Sometimes the black vitalium wings were spread, to catch the energy of the sun. The sunship draws its name from the fact that it is driven by solar power. It utilizes the remarkable properties of the rare radioactive metal, vitalium, which is believed to be the very basis of life, since it was first discovered to exist in minute traces in those complex substances so necessary to all life, the vitamins. Large deposits were discovered at Kepler and elsewhere on the moon during the twenty-first century. Under the sun's rays vitalium undergoes a change to triatomic form, storing up the vast energy of sunlight. The vitalium plates from the sunshine are built into batteries with alternate sheets of copper, from which the solar energy may be drawn in the form of electric current. As the battery discharges, the vitalium reverts to its stabler allotropic form, and may be used again and again. The Vitalium Power Company's plants in Arizona, Chili, Australia, the Sahara, and the Gobi now furnish most of the earth's power. The sunship, recharging its vitalium batteries in space, can cruise indefinitely.

It was on the fifth day out from Lakehurst. The *Fury*, with her sister ships spread out some thousands of miles to right and left, was cruising at five thousand miles per hour, at heliocentric elevation 93.-243546, ecliptic declination 7° 18' 46" north, right ascension XIX hours, 20 min., 31 sec. The earth was a little green globe beside her, and the moon a thin silver crescent beyond.

"Object ahead!" called a lookout in the domed pilot-house of the *Fury*, turning from his telescope to where Captain Brand and Bill stood smoking, comfortably held to the floor by the ship's acceleration. "In Scorpio, about five degrees above Antares. Distance fifteen thousand miles. It seems to be round and blue."

"The Prince, at last," Brand chuckled, an eager grin on his square chinned face, light of battle flashing in his blue eyes.

He gave orders that set the heliographic mirrors flickering signals for all nine of the Moon Patrol fliers to converge about the strange object, in a great crescent. The black fins that carried the charging vitalium plates were drawn in, and the full power of the motor ray tubes thrown on, to drive ahead each slender silver flier at the limit of her acceleration.

Four telescopes from the *Fury* were turned upon the strange object. Captain Brand and Bill took turns peering through one of them. When Bill looked, he saw the infinite black gulf of space, silvered with star-dust of distant nebulae. Hanging in the blackness was an azure sphere, gleaming bright as a great globe cut from turquoise. Bill was reminded of a similar blue globe he had seen—when he had stood at the enormous telescope on Trainor's Tower, and watched a little blue circle against the red deserts of Mars.

Brand took two or three observations, figured swiftly.

"It's moving," he said. "About fourteen thousand miles per hour. Funny. It is moving directly toward the earth, almost from the direction of the planet Mars. I wonder—" He seized the pencil, figured again. "Queer. That thing seems headed for the earth, from a point on the orbit of

Mars, where that planet was about forty days ago. Do you suppose the Martians are paying us a visit?"

"Then it's not the Prince of Space?"

"I don't know. Its direction might be just a coincidence. And the Prince might be a Martian, for all I know. Anyhow, we're going to find what that blue globe is!"

Two hours later the nine sunships were drawn up in the form of a great half circle, closing swiftly on the blue globe, which had been calculated to be about one hundred feet in diameter. The sunships were nearly a thousand miles from the globe, and scattered along a curved line two thousand miles in length. Captain Brand gave orders for eight forward tubes on each flier to be made ready for use as weapons. From his own ship he flashed a heliographic signal.

"The *Fury*, of the Moon Patrol, demands that you show ship's papers, identification tags for all passengers, and submit to search for contraband."

The message was three times repeated, but no reply came from the azure globe. It continued on its course. The slender white sunships came plunging swiftly toward it, until the crescent they formed was not two hundred miles between the points, the blue globe not a hundred miles from the war-fliers.

Then Bill, with his eye at a telescope, saw a little spark of purple light appear beside the blue globe. A tiny, bright point of violet-red fire with a white line running from it, back to the center of the sphere. The purple spark grew, the white line lengthened. Abruptly, the newspaperman realized that the purple was an object hurtling toward him with incredible speed.

Even as the realization burst upon him, the spark became visible as a little red-blue sphere, brightly luminous. A white beam shone behind it, seemed to push it with ever-increasing velocity. The purple globe shot past, vanished. The white ray snapped out.

"A weapon!" he exclaimed.

"A weapon and a warning," said Brand, still peering through another eyepiece. "And we reply!"

"Heliograph!" he shouted into a speaking tube. "Each ship will open with one forward tube, operating one second twelve times per minute. Increase power of rear tubes to compensate repulsion."

White shields flickered. Blindingly brilliant rays, straight bars of dazzling opalescence, burst intermittently from each of the nine ships, striking across a hundred miles of space to batter the blue globe with a hail of charged atoms.

Again a purple spark appeared from the sapphire globe, with a beam of white fire behind it. A tiny purple globe, hurtling at an inconceivable velocity before a lance of white flame. It reached out, with a certain deliberation, yet too quickly for a man to do more than see it.

It struck a sunship, at one tip of the crescent formation.

A dazing flash of violet flame burst out. The tiny globe seemed to explode into a huge flare of red-blue light. And where the slim, eight-sided ship had been was a crushed and twisted mass of metal.

"A solid projectile!" Brand cried. "And driven on the positive ray! Our experts have tried it, but the ray always exploded the shell. And that was some explosion! I don't know what—unless atomic energy."

The eight sunships that remained were closing swiftly upon the blue globe. The dazzling white rays flashed intermittently from them. They struck the blue globe squarely—the fighting crews of the Moon Patrol are trained until their rays are directed with deadly accuracy. The azure sphere, unharmed, shone with bright radiance—it seemed that a thin mist of glittering blue particles was gathering about it, like a dust of powdered sapphires.

Another purple spark leapt from the turquoise globe.

In the time that it took a man's eyes to move from globe to slim, glistening sunship, the white ray had driven the purple spark across the distance. Another vivid flash of violet light. And another sunship became a hurtling mass of twisted wreckage.

"We are seven," Brand quoted grimly.

"Heliograph!" he shouted into the mouthpiece. "Fire all forward tubes one second twenty times a minute. Increase rear power to maximum."

White rays burst from the seven darting sunships, flashing off and on. That sapphire globe grew bright, with a strange luminosity. The thin mist of sparkling blue particles seemed to grow more dense about it.

"Our rays don't seem to be doing any good," Brand muttered, puzzled. "The blue about that globe must be some sort of vibratory screen."

Another purple spark, with the narrow white line of fire behind it, swept across to the flier from the opposite horn of the crescent, burst into a sheet of blinding red-violet light. Another ship was a twisted mass of metal.

"Seven no longer..." Brand called grimly to Bill.

"Looks as if the Prince has got us beaten!" the reporter cried.

"Not while a ship can fight!" exclaimed the Captain. "This is the Moon Patrol!" Another tiny purple globe traced its line of light across the black, star-misted sky.

Another sunship crumpled in a violet flash.

"They're picking 'em off the ends," Bill observed. "We're in the middle, so I guess we're last."

"Then," said Captain Brand, "we've got time to ram 'em."

"Control!" he shouted into the speaking tube. "Cut off forward tubes and make all speed for the enemy. Heliograph! Fight to the end! I am going to ram them!"

Another red-blue spark moved with its quick deliberation. A purple flash left another ship in twisted ruin.

Bill took his eye from the telescope. The blue globe, bright under the rays, with the sapphire mist sparkling about it, was only twenty miles away. He could see it with his naked eye, drifting swiftly among the familiar stars of Scorpio.

It grew larger very swiftly.

With the quickness of thought, the purple sparks moved out alternately to right and to left. They never missed. Each one exploded in purple flame, crushed a sunship.

"Three fliers left," Bill counted, eyes on the growing blue globe before them. "Two left. Good-by, Brand." He grasped the bluff Captain's hand. "One left. Will we have time?"

He looked forward. The blue globe, with the dancing, sparkling haze of sapphire swirling about it, was swiftly expanding.

"The last one! Our turn now!"

He saw a tiny fleck of purple light dart out of the expanding azure sphere that they had hoped to ram. Then red-violet flame seemed to envelope him. He felt the floor of the bridge tremble beneath his feet. He heard the beginning of a shivering crash like that of shattering glass. Then the world was mercifully dark and still.

CHAPTER THREE
The City of Space

Bill lay on an Alpine glacier, a painful broken leg inextricably wedged in a crevasse. It was dark, frightfully cold. In vain he struggled to move, to seek light and warmth, while the grim grip of the ice held him, while bitter wind howled about him and the piercing cold of the blizzard crept numbingly up his limbs.

He came to with a start, realized that it was a dream. But he was none the less freezing, gasping for thin frigid air, that somehow would not come into his lungs. All about was darkness. He lay on cold metal.

"In the wreck of the *Fury!*" he thought. "The air is leaking out. And the cold of space. A frozen tomb..."

He must have made a sound, for a groan came from beside him. He fought to draw breath, tried to speak. He choked, and his voice was oddly high and thin.

"Who are—"

He ended in a fit of coughing, felt warm blood spraying from his mouth. Faintly he heard a whisper beside him.

"I'm Brand. The Moon Patrol—fought to the last—"

Bill could speak no more, and evidently the redoubtable captain could not. For a long time they lay in freezing silence. Bill had no hope of life, he felt only very grim satisfaction in the fact that he and Brand had not been killed outright.

But suddenly he was thrilled with hope. He heard a crash of hammer blows upon metal, sharp as the sound of snapping glass in the thin air. Then he heard the thin hiss of an oxygen lance.

Someone was cutting a way to them through the wreckage. Only a moment later, it seemed, a vivid bar of light cleft the darkness, searched the wrecked bridge, settled upon the two limp figures. Bill saw grotesque figures in cumbrous metal space suits clambering through a hole they had cut. He felt an oxygen helmet being fastened about his head, heard the thin hiss of the escaping gas, and was once more able to breathe.

Again he slipped into oblivion.

He awoke with the sensation that infinite time had passed. He sat up quickly, feeling strong, alert, fully recovered in every faculty, a clear memory of every detail of the disastrous encounter with the strange blue globe-ship springing instantly to his mind.

He was in a clean bed in a little white-walled room. Captain Brand, a surprised grin on his bluff, rough-hewn features, was sitting upon another bed beside him. Two attendants in white uniform stood just inside the door and a nervous little man in black suit, evidently a doctor, was hastily replacing gleaming instruments in a leather bag.

A tall man appeared suddenly in the door, clad in a striking uniform of black, scarlet, and gold-black trousers, scarlet military coat and cap, gold buttons and decorations. He carried in his hand a glittering positive ray pistol.

"Gentlemen," he said in a crisp, gruff voice, "you may consider yourselves prisoners of the Prince of Space."

"How come?" Brand demanded.

"The Prince was kind enough to have you removed from the wreck of your ship, and brought aboard the *Red Rover,* his own sunship. You have been kept unconscious until your recovery was complete."

"And what do you want with us now?" Brand was rather aggressive.

The man with the pistol smiled. "That, gentlemen, I am happy to say, rests largely with yourselves."

"I am an officer in the Moon Patrol," said Brand. "I prefer death to anything-"

"Wait, Captain. You need have none but the kindest feelings for my master, the Prince of Space. I now ask you nothing but your word as an officer and a gentleman that you will act as becomes a guest of the Prince. Your promise will lose you nothing and win you much."

"Very good, I promise," Brand agreed after a moment. "—for twenty-four hours."

He pulled out his watch, looked at it. The man in the door lowered his pistol, smiling, and walked across to shake hands with Brand.

"Call me Smith," he introduced himself. "Captain of the Prince's cruiser, *Red Rover.*"

Still smiling, he beckoned toward the door.

"And if you like, gentlemen, you may come with me to the bridge. The *Red Rover* is to land in an hour."

Brand sprang nimbly to the floor, and Bill followed. The flier was maintaining a moderate acceleration—they felt light, but were able to walk without difficulty. Beyond the door was a round shaft, with a ladder through its length. Captain Smith clambered up the ladder. Brand and Bill swung up behind him.

After an easy climb of fifty feet or so, they entered a domed pilothouse, with vitrolite observation panels, telescopes, maps and charts, and speaking tube—an arrangement similar to that of the *Fury.*

Black, star-strewn heavens lay before them. Bill looked for the earth, found it visible in the periscopic screens almost behind them. It was a little green disk, the moon but a white dot beside it.

"We land in an hour," he exclaimed.

"I didn't say where," said Captain Smith, smiling. "Our landing place is a million miles from the earth."

"Not on earth? Then where—"

"At the City of Space."

"The City of Space?"

"The capital of the Prince of Space. It is not a thousand miles before us."

Bill peered ahead, through the vitrolite dome, distinguished the bright constellation of Sagittarius with the luminous clouds of the Galaxy behind it.

"I don't see anything—"

"The Prince does not care to advertise his city. The outside of the City of Space is covered with black vitalium— which furnishes us with power. Reflecting none of the sun's rays, it cannot be seen by reflected light. Against the black background of space it is invisible, except when it occults a star."

Captain Smith busied himself with giving orders for the landing. Bill and Brand stood for many minutes looking forward through the vitrolite dome, while the motor ray tubes retarded the flier. Presently a little black point came against the silver haze of the Milky Way. It grew, stars vanishing behind its rim, until a huge section of the heavens was utterly black before them.

"The City of Space is in a cylinder," Captain Smith said. "Roughly five thousand feet in diameter, and about that high. It is built largely of meteoric iron, which we captured from a meteorite swarm, making navigation safe and getting useful metal at the same time. The cylinder whirls constantly, with such speed that the centrifugal force against the sides equals the force of gravity on the earth. The city is built around the inside of the cylinder—so that one can look up and see his neighbor's house apparently upside down, a mile above his head. We enter through a lock in one end of the cylinder."

A vast disk of dull black metal was now visible a few yards outside the vitrolite panels. A huge metal valve swung open in it, revealing a bright space beyond. The *Red Rover* moved into the chamber, the mighty valve closed behind her, air hissed in about her, an inner valve was opened, and she slipped into the City of Space.

They were, Bill saw, at the center of an enormous cylinder. The sides, half a mile away, above and below them, were covered with buildings along neat, tree-bordered streets, scattered with green lawns, tiny gardens, and bits of wooded park. It seemed very strange to Bill, to see these endless streets about the inside of a tube, so that one by walking a little over three miles in one direction would arrive again at the starting point, in the same way that one gets back to the starting point after going around the earth in one direction.

At the ends of the cylinder, fastened to the huge metal disks, which closed the ends, were elaborate and complex mechanisms, machines strange and massive. "They must be for heating the city," Bill thought, "and for purifying the air, for furnishing light and power, perhaps even for moving it about." The leek through which they had entered was part of this mechanism.

In the center of each end of the cylinder hung a huge light, seeming large and round as the sun, flooding the place with brilliant mellow rays.

"There are five thousand people here," said Captain Smith. "The Prince has always kept the best specimens among his captives, and others have been recruited besides. We are self-sustaining as the earth is. We use the power of the sun—through our vitalium batteries. We grow our own food. We utilize our waste products—matter here goes through a regular cycle of life and death as on the earth. Men eat food containing carbon, breathe in oxygen, and breathe out carbon dioxide; our plants break up the carbon dioxide, make more foods containing the same carbon, and give off the oxygen for men to breathe again. Our nitrogen, or oxygen and hydrogen, go through similar cycles. The power of the sun is all we need from outside."

Captain Smith guided his "guests" down the ladder, and out through the ship's airlock. They entered an elevator.

Three minutes later they stepped off upon the side of the great cylinder that housed the City, and entered a low building with a broad concrete road curving up before it. As they stepped out, it gave Bill a curious dizzy feeling to look up and see busy streets, inverted, a mile above his head. The road before them curved smoothly up on either hand, bordered with beautiful trees, until its ends met again above his head.

The centrifugal force that held objects against the sides of the cylinder acted in precisely the same way as gravity on the earth—except that it pulled away from the center of the cylinder, instead of toward it.

A glistening heliocar came skimming down upon whirling heliocopters, dropped to rubber tires, and rolled up beside them. A young man of military bearing, clad in a striking uniform of red, black, and gold, stepped out, saluted stiffly.

"Captain Smith," he said, "the Prince desires your attendance at his private office immediately with your guests."

Smith motioned Bill and Captain Brand into the richly upholstered body of the heliocar. Bill, gazing up at the end of the huge cylinder with a city inside it, caught sight, for the first time, of the exterior of the *Red Rover,* the ship that had brought them to the City of Space. It lay just beside the massive machinery of the air lock, supported in a heavy metal cradle, with the elevator tube running straight from it to the building behind them.

"Look, Brand," Bill gasped. "That isn't the blue globe. It isn't the ship we fought at all!"

Brand looked. The *Red Rover* was much the same sort of ship that the *Fury* had been. She was slender and tapering, cigar-shaped, some two hundred feet in length and twenty-five in diameter—nearly twice as large as the *Fury.* She was cylindrical, instead of octagonal, and she mounted twenty-four motor tubes, in two rings fore and aft, of twelve each, instead of eight.

Brand turned to Smith. "How's this?" he demanded. "Where is the blue globe? Did you have two ships?"

A smile flickered over Smith's stern face. "You have a revelation waiting for you. But it is better not to keep the Prince waiting."

They stepped into the heliocar. The pilot sprang to his place, set the electric motors whirring. The machine rolled easily forward, took the air on spinning helicopters. The road, lined with green gardens and bright cottages, dropped away "below" them, and other houses drew nearer "above." In the center of the cylinder the young man dexterously inverted the flier and they continued on a straight line toward an imposing concrete building, which now seemed "below."

The heliocar landed; they sprang out and approached the imposing building of several stories. Guards uniformed in scarlet, black and gold standing just outside the door held ray pistols in readiness. Smith hurried his "guests" past; they entered a long, high-ceilinged room. It gave a first impression of stately luxury. The walls were paneled with rich dark wood, hung with a few striking paintings. It was almost empty of furniture; a heavy desk stood alone toward the farther end. A tall young man rose from behind this desk, advanced rapidly to meet them.

"My guests, sir," said Smith. "Captain Brand of the *Fury*, and a reporter."

"The mysterious Mr. Cain," Bill gasped.

Indeed, Mr. Cain stood before him, a tall man, slender and wiry, with a certain not unhandsome sternness in his dark face. A smile twinkled in his black, enigmatic eyes—which none the less looked as if they might easily flash with fierce authority.

"And Mr. Win—or, I believe you asked me to call you Bill. You seem a very hard man to evade."

Still smiling enigmatically, Mr. Cain took Bill's hand, and then shook hands with Captain Brand.

"But—are you the Prince of Space?" Bill demanded.

"I am. Cain was only a *nom de guerre,* so to speak. Gentlemen, I welcome you to the City of Space!"

"And you kidnapped yourself?"

"My men brought the *Red Rover* for me."

"Dr. Trainor and his daughter—" Bill ejaculated.

"They are friends of mine. They are here."

"And that blue globe," said Captain Brand. "What was that?"

"You saw the course it was following?"

"It was headed to intersect the orbit of the earth—and its direction was on a line that cuts the orbit of Mars where that planet was forty days ago."

The Prince turned to Bill. "And you have seen something like that blue globe before?"

"Why, yes. The little blue circle on Mars—that I saw through the great telescope on Trainor's Tower."

A sober smile flickered across the dark lean face of the Prince.

"Then, gentlemen, you should believe me. The earth is threatened with a dreadful danger from Mars. The blue globe that wrecked your fleet was a ship from Mars. It was another Martian flier that took the *Helicon.* I believe I have credit for that ghastly exploit of sucking out the passengers' blood." His smile became grimly humorous. "One of the consequences of my position."

"Martian fliers?" echoed Captain Brand. "Then how did we come to be on your ship?"

"I haven't any weapon that will meet those purple atomic bombs on equal terms—though we are now working out a new device. I had Smith cruising around the blue globe in our *Red Rover* to see what he could learn. He was investigating the wrecks, and found you alive."

"You really mean that men from Mars have come this near the earth?" Captain Brand was frankly incredulous.

"Not men," the Prince corrected, smiling. "But *things* from Mars have done it. They have already landed on earth, in fact."

He turned to the desk, picked up a broad sheet of cardboard.

"I have a color photograph here."

Bill studied it, saw that it looked like an aerial photograph of a vast stretch of mountain and desert, a monotonous expanse of gray, tinged with green and red.

"A photograph, taken from space, of part of the state of Chihuahua, Mexico. And see!"

He pointed to a little blue disk in the green-gray expanse of a plain, just below a narrow mountain ridge, with the fine green line that marked a river just beside it.

"That blue circle is the first ship that came. It was the things aboard it that sucked the blood out of the people on the *Helicon.*"

Captain Brand was staring at the tall, smiling man, with a curious expression on his red, square-chinned face. Suddenly he spoke.

"Your Highness, or whatever we must call you—"

"Just call me Prince. Cain is not my name. Once I had a name—but now I am nameless."

The thin dark face suddenly lined with pain, the lips closed in a narrow line. The Prince swept a hand across his high forehead, as if to sweep something unpleasant away.

"Well, Prince, I'm with you. That is, if you want an officer from the Moon Patrol." A sheepish smile overspread his bluff features. "I would have killed a man for suggesting that

I would ever do such a thing. But I'll fight for you as well as I ever did for the honor of the Patrol."

"Thanks, Brand." The Prince took his hand, smiling again.

"Count me in too, of course," said Bill.

"Both of you will be valuable men," said the Prince.

He picked up a sheaf of papers, scanned them quickly, seemed to mark off one item from a sheet and add another.

"The *Red Rover* sets out for the earth in one hour, gentlemen. We're going to try a surprise attack on that blue globe in the desert. You will both go aboard."

"And I'm going too!" A woman's voice, soft and a little husky, spoke beside them. Recognizing it, Bill turned to see Paula Trainor standing behind them, an eager smile on her elfinly beautiful face. Her amazing eyes were fixed upon the Prince, their brown depths filled, for the moment, with passionate wistful yearning.

"Why, no, Paula," the Prince said. "It's dangerous."

Tears swam mistily in the golden orbs. "I will go! I must! I must!" The girl cried out the words, a sobbing catch in her voice.

"Very well, then," the Prince agreed, smiling absently. "Your father will be along of course. But anything will be likely to happen."

"But you will be there in danger, too," cried the girl.

"We start in an hour," said the Prince. "Smith, you may take Brand and Windsor back aboard the *Red Rover.*"

"Curse his fatherly indifference," Bill muttered under his breath as they walked out through the guarded door. "Can't he see that she loves him?"

Smith must have heard him, for he turned to him, spoke confidentially. "The Prince is a determined misogynist. I think an unfortunate love affair was what ruined his life—back on the earth. He left his history, even his name, behind him. I think a woman was the trouble. He won't look at a woman now."

They were outside again, startled anew by the amazing scene of a street of houses and gardens that curved evenly up on either side of them and met above, so that men were moving about, head downward directly above them.

The heliocar was waiting. The three got aboard, were lifted and swiftly carried to the slender silver cylinder of the *Red Rover,* where it hung among the ponderous machinery of the air lock, on the end of the huge cylinder that housed the amazing City of Space.

"I will show you your rooms," said Captain Smith. "And in an hour we are off to attack the Martians in Mexico."

CHAPTER FOUR
Vampires in the Desert

Forty hours later the *Red Rover* entered the atmosphere of the earth, above northern Mexico. It was night, the desert was shrouded in blackness. The telescopes revealed only the lights at ranches scattered as thinly as they had been two centuries before.

Bill was in the bridge-room, with Captain Smith.

"The blue globe that destroyed your fleet has already landed here," Smith said. "We saw both of them before they slipped into the shadow of night. They were right together, and it seems that a white metal building has been set up between them."

"The Prince means to attack? In spite of those purple atomic bombs?" Bill seemed surprised.

"Yes. They are below a low mountain ridge. We land on the other side of the hill, a dozen miles off, and give 'em a surprise at dawn."

"We'd better be careful," Bill said doubtfully. "They're more likely to surprise us. If you had been in front of one of those little purple bombs, flying on the white ray…"

"We have a sort of rocket torpedo that Doc Trainor invented. The Prince means to try that on 'em."

The *Red Rover* dropped swiftly, with Smith's skilled hands on the controls. It seemed but a few minutes until the dark shadow of the earth beneath abruptly resolved itself into a level plain scattered with looming shapes that were clumps of mesquite and sagebrush. The slim silver cylinder came silently to rest upon the desert, beneath stars that shone clearly, though to Bill they seemed dim in comparison with the splendid wonders of space.

Three hours before dawn, five men slipped out through the air lock. The Prince himself was the leader, with Captains Brand and Smith, Bill, and a young officer named Walker. Each man carried a searchlight and a positive ray pistol. And strapped upon the back of each was a rocket torpedo—a smooth, white metal tube, four feet long and as many inches thick, weighing some eighty pounds.

Dr. Trainor, kindly, bald-headed old scientist, was left in charge of the ship. He and his daughter came out of the air lock into the darkness, to bid the five adventurers farewell.

"We should be back by night," said the Prince, his even white teeth flashing in the darkness. "Wait for us until then. If we don't come, return at once to the City of Space. I want no one to follow us, and no attempt made to rescue us if we don't come back. If we aren't back by tomorrow night we shall be dead."

"Very good, sir," Trainor nodded.

"I'm coming with you, then," Paula declared suddenly.

"Absolutely you are not!" cried the Prince. "Dr. Trainor, I command you not to let your daughter off the ship until we return."

Paula turned quickly away, a slim pillar of misty white in the darkness. Bill heard a little choking sound; he knew that she had burst into teals.

"I can't let you go off into such danger, without me," she cried, almost hysterical. "I can't!"

The Prince swung a heavy torpedo higher on his shoulders, and strode off over bare gravel toward the low rocky slope of the mountain that lay to northward, faintly revealed in the light of the stars. The other four followed silently. The slender sunship, with the old scientist and his sobbing daughter outside the air lock, quickly vanished behind them.

With only an occasional cautious flicker of the flashlights the five men picked their way over bare hard ground, among scattered clumps of mesquite. Presently they crossed a barren lava bed, clambering over huge blocks of twisted black volcanic rock. Up the slope of the mountain they struggled, sweating under heavy burdens, blundering into spiky cactus, stumbling over boulders and sagebrush.

When the silver and rose of dawn came in the purple eastern sky, the five lay on bare rock at the top of the low ridge, overlooking the flat, mesquite-covered valley beyond. The valley floor was a brownish green in the light of morning, the hills that rose far across it a hazy blue-gray, faintly tinged with green on age-worn slopes.

Like a string of emeralds dropped down the valley lay an endless wandering line of cottonwoods, of a light and vivid green that stood out from the somber plain. These trees traced the winding course of a stream, the Rio Casas Grandes.

Lying against the cottonwoods, and rising above their tops, were two great spheres of blue, gleaming like twin globes of lapis lazuli in the morning light. They were not far apart, and between them rose a curious domed structure of white, silvery metal.

Each of the five men lifted his heavy metal tube, leveled it across a boulder before him. The Prince, alert and smiling despite the dust and stain of the march through the desert, spoke to the others.

"This little tube along the top of the torpedo is a telescope sight. You will peer through, get the cross hairs squarely upon your target, and hold them there. Then press this nickeled lever. That starts the projectile inside the case to spinning so that inertia will hold it true. Then, being certain that the aim is correct, press the red button. The torpedo is thrown from the case by compressed air, and a positive ray mechanism drives it true to the target. When it strikes, about fifty pounds of Dr. Trainor's new explosive, *trainite,* will be set off.

"Walker, you and Windsor take the right globe. Smith and Brand, the left. I'll have a shot at that peculiar edifice between them."

Bill balanced his torpedo, peered through the telescope, and pressed the lever. The hum of a motor came from the heavy tube.

"All ready?" the Prince inquired.

"Ready," each man returned.

"Fire!"

Bill pressed the red button. The tube drove heavily backward in his hands, and then was but a light, sheet-metal shell. He saw a little gleam of white light before him, against the right blue globe, a diminishing point. It was the motor ray that drove the torpedo speeding toward its mark.

Great flares of orange light hid the two azure spheres and the white dome between them. The spheres and the dome crumpled and vanished, and a thin haze of bluish smoke swirled about them.

"Good shooting!" the Prince commented. "This motor torpedo of Trainor's ought to put a lot of the old fighting equipment in the museum—if we were disposed to bestow such a dangerous toy upon humanity.

"But let's get over and see what happened."

Grasping ray pistols, they sprang to their feet and plunged down the rocky slope. It was five miles to the river. Nearly two hours later it was, when the five men slipped out of the mesquites, to look two hundred yards across an open, grassy flat to the wall of green trees along the river

Three great heaps of wreckage lay upon the flat. At the right and the left were crumpled masses of bright silver metal—evidently the remains of the globes. In the center was another pile of bent and twisted metal, which had been the domed building.

"Funny that those blue globes look like ordinary white metal now," said Smith.

"I wonder if the blue is not some sort of etheric screen?" Brand commented. "When we were fighting, our rays seemed to take no effect. It occurred to me that some vibratory wall might have stopped them."

"It's possible," the Prince agreed. "I'll take up the possibilities with Trainor. If they have such a screen, it might even be opaque to gravity. Quite a convenience in maneuvering a ship."

As they spoke, they were advancing cautiously, stopping to pick up bits of white metal that had been scattered about by the explosion.

Suddenly Bill's eyes caught movement from the pile of crumpled metal that had been the white dome. It seemed that a green plant was growing quickly from among the ruins. Green tendrils shot up amazingly. Then he saw on the end of a twisted stalk a glowing purple thing that looked somehow like an eye.

At first sight of the thing he had stopped in amazement, leveling his deadly ray pistol and shouting, "Look out!"

Before the shout had died in his throat, before the others had time to turn their heads, they caught the flash of metal among the twining green tentacles. The thing was lifting a metal object.

Then Bill saw a tiny purple spark dart from a bright little mechanism that the green tendrils held. He saw a blinding flash of violet light. His consciousness was cut off abruptly.

The next he knew he was lying on his back on rocky soil. He felt considerably bruised and battered, and his right eye was swollen so that he could not open it. Struggling to a sitting position, he found his hands and feet bound by bloody manacles of unfamiliar design. Captain Brand was lying on his elbow beside him, half under the thin shade of a mesquite bush. Brand looked much torn and disheveled; blood was streaming across his face from a gash in his scalp. His hands and feet also were bound with fetters of white metal.

"What happened?" Bill called dazedly.

"Not so loud," Brand whispered. "The thing—a Martian left alive, I guess it is. Must have been somewhere out in the brush when we shot. It blew us up with an atomic bomb. Smith and Walker dead—blown to pieces."

"And the Prince?"

"I can speak for myself."

Hearing the familiar low voice, Bill turned. He saw the Prince squatted down, in the blazing sunshine, hands and feet manacled, hat off and face covered with blood and grime.

"Was it that—that green thing?" Bill asked.

"Looks like a sort of animated plant," said the Prince. "A bunch of green tentacles, that it uses for hands. Three purple eyes on green stalks. Just enough of a body to join it all together. Not like anything I ever saw. But the Martians, originating under different conditions, ought to be different."

"What is going to happen now?" Bill inquired.

"Probably it will suck our blood—as it did to the passengers of the *Helicon,*" Brand suggested grimly.

Windsor fell silent. It was almost noon. The desert sun was very hot. The motionless air was oppressive with a dry, parching heat; and flies buzzed annoyingly about his bleeding cuts. Wrists and ankles ached under the cruel pressure of the manacles.

"Wish the thing would come back, and end the suspense," Brand muttered.

Bill reflected with satisfaction that he had no relatives to be saddened by his demise. He had no great fear of death. Newspaper work in the twenty-second century is not all commonplace monotony; your veteran reporter is pretty well inured to danger.

"Glad I haven't anyone to worry about me," he observed.

"So am I," the Prince said bitterly. "I left them all, years ago."

"But you have someone," Bill cried. "It isn't my business to say it, but that makes no difference now. And you're a fool not to know. Paula Trainor loves you! This will kill her!"

The Prince looked up, a bitter smile visible behind the bloody grime on his thin dark face.

"Paula—in love with me! We're friends, of course. But love? I used to believe in love. I have not been always a nameless outcast of space. Once I had name, family—even wealth and position. I trusted my name and my honor to a beautiful woman. I loved her! She said she loved me—I thought she meant it. She used me for a tool. I was trustful; she was clever."

The dark eyes of the Prince burned in fierce anger.

"When she was through with me she left me to die in disgrace. I barely escaped with my life. She had robbed me of my name, wealth, position. She named me the outlaw. She made me appear a traitor to those who trusted me—then laughed at me. She laughed at me and called me a fool. I was—but I won't be again!

"At first I was filled with anger at the whole world, at the unjust laws and the silly conventions and the cruel intolerance of men. I became the pirate of space. A pariah. Fighting against my own kind. Struggling desperately for power."

For a few moments he was moodily silent, slapping at the flies that buzzed around his bloody wounds.

"I gained power. And I learned of the dangers from Mars. First I was glad. Glad to see the race of man swept out. Parasites men seemed. Insects. Life—what is it but a kind of decay on a mote in space? Then I got a saner view, and built the City of Space, to save a few men. Then because the few seemed to have noble qualities, I resolved to try to save the world.

"But it is too late. We have lost. And I have had enough of love, enough of women, with their soft, alluring bodies, and the sweet lying voices, and the heartless scheming."

The Prince fell into black silence, motionless, heedless of the flies that swarmed about him. Presently Brand contrived, despite his manacles, to fish a packet of cigarettes from his pocket, extract one, and tossed the others to Bill, who managed to light one for the Prince. The three battered men sat in dazzling sun and blistering heat, smoking and trying to forget heat and flies and torturing manacles—and the death that loomed so near.

It was early noon when Bill heard a little rustling beyond the mesquites. In a moment the Martian appeared. A grotesque and terrifying being it was. Scores of green tentacles, slender and writhing, grew from an insignificant body. Three lidless, purple eyes, staring, alien, and malevolent, watched them alertly from foot-long green stalks that rose above the body. The creature half walked on tentacles extended below it, half dragged itself along by green appendages that reached out to grasp mesquite limbs above it. One inch-thick coil carried a curious instrument of glittering crystal and white metal—it was a strange, gleaming thing, remotely like a ray pistol. And fastened about another tentacle was a little metal ring, from which an odd-looking little bar dangled.

The thing came straight for the Prince. Bill screamed a warning. The Prince saw it, twisted himself over on the ground, tried desperately to crawl away. The thing reached out a slender tentacle, many yards long. It grasped him about the neck, drew him back.

In a moment the dreadful being was crouching in a writhing green mass above the body of the manacled man. Once he screamed piteously, then there was no sound save loud, gasping breaths. His muscles knotted as he struggled in agony against the fetters and the coils of the monster.

Bill and Captain Brand lay there, unable either to escape or to give assistance. In silent horror they watched the scene. They saw that each slender green tentacle ended in a sharp-edged suction disk. They watched the disks forcing themselves against the throat of the agonized man, tearing a way through his clothing to his body. They saw constrictions move down the rubber-like green tentacles as if they were sucking, while red drops oozed out about the edge of the disks.

"Our turn next," muttered Captain Brand.

"And after us, the world," Bill breathed, tense with horror.

A narrow, white beam, blindingly brilliant, flashed from beyond the dull green foliage of the mesquite. It struck the crouching monster waveringly. Without a sound, it leapt, flinging itself aside from the body of the Prince. It raised its curious weapon. A tiny purple spark darted from it.

A shattering crash rang out at a little distance. There was a thin scream—a woman's scream.

Then the white ray stabbed at the monster again, and it collapsed in a twitching heap of thin green coils, upon the still body of the Prince.

A slender girl rushed out of the brush, tossed aside a ray pistol, and flung herself upon the monster, trying to drag it from the Prince. It was Paula Trainor. Her clothing was torn. Her skin was scratched and bleeding from miles of running through the desert of rocks and cactus and thorny mesquite. She was evidently exhausted. But she flung herself with desperate energy to the rescue of the injured man.

The body of the dead thing was light enough. But the sucking disks still clung to the flesh. They pulled and tore it when she tugged at them. She struggled desperately to drag them loose, by turns sobbing and laughing hysterically.

"If you can help us get loose, we might help," Bill suggested.

The girl raised a piteous face. "Oh, Mr. Bill—Captain Brand! Is he dead?"

"I think not, Miss Paula. The thing had just jumped on him. Buck up!"

"See the little bar—it looks like a sliver of aluminum— fastened to the metal ring about that coil?" Brand said. "It might be the key for these chains. End of it seems to be shaped about right. Suppose you try it?"

In nervous haste, the girl tore the little bar from its ring. With Brand's aid, she was able to unlock his fetters. The Captain lost no time in freeing Bill and removing the manacles from the unconscious Prince.

The thin, rubber-like tentacles could not be torn loose. Brand cut them with his knife. He found them tough and fibrous. Red blood flowed from them when they were severed.

Bill carried the injured man down to the shade of the cottonwoods, brought water to him in a hat from the muddy little stream below. In a few minutes he was conscious, though weak from loss of blood.

Captain Brand, after satisfying himself that Paula had killed the Martian, and that it was the only one that had survived in the wreckage of the blue globes and the metal dome, set off to cross the mountain and bring back the sunship.

When the *Red Rover* came into view late that evening, a beautiful slender bar of silver against the pyrotechnic gold and scarlet splendor of the desert sunset, the Prince of Space was hobbling about, supported on Bill's arm, examining the wreckage of the Martian fliers.

Paula was hovering eagerly about him, anxious to aid him. Bill noticed the pain and despair that clouded her brown eyes. She had been holding the Prince's head in her arms when he regained consciousness. Her lips had been very close to his, and bright tears were brimming in her golden eyes.

Bill had seen the Prince push her away, then thank her gruffly when he had found what she had done.

"Paula, you have done a great thing for the world," Bill had heard him say.

"It wasn't the world at all. It was for you," the girl had cried, tearfully.

She had turned away, to hide her tears. And the Prince had said nothing more.

The *Red Rover* landed beside the wreckage of the Martian fliers. After a few hours spent in examining and photographing the wrecks, in taking specimens of the white alloy of which they were built, and of other substances used in the construction, they all went back on the sunship, taking the dead Martian and other objects for further study. Brand took off for the upper atmosphere.

"Captain Brand," the Prince said as they stood in the bridge room, "since the death of poor Captain Smith this morning, I believe you are the most skillful sunship officer in my organization. Hereafter you are in command of the *Red Rover*, with Harris and Vincent as your officers.

"We have a huge task before us. The victory we have won is but the first hand in the game that decides the fate of Earth."

CHAPTER FIVE
The Triton's Treasure

"I must have at least two tons of vitalium," the Prince of Space told Bill, when the newspaperman came to the bridge of the *Red Rover* after twenty hours in the bunk. The Prince was pale and weak from loss of blood, but seemed to suffer no other ill effects from his encounter with the Martian.

"Two tons of vitalium," Bill exclaimed. "A small demand! I doubt if there is that much on the market, if you had all the Confederation's treasury to buy it with."

"I must have it, and at once! I am going to fit out the *Red Rover* for a voyage to Mars. It will take that much vitalium for the batteries."

"We are going to Mars?"

"The only hope for humanity is for us to strike first and to strike hard."

"If the world knew of the danger, we could get help."

"That's where you come in. I told you that I should need publicity. It is your business to tell the public about things. I want you to tell humanity about the danger from Mars. Make it convincing and make it strong. Say anything you like so long as you leave the Prince of Space out of it. I have the body of the Martian that attacked me preserved in alcohol. You have that and the wreckage in the desert to substantiate your story. I will land you at Trainor's Tower in New York tonight. You will have twenty-four hours to convince the world, and raise two tons of vitalium. It has to be done!"

"A big order," Bill said doubtfully. "But I'll do my best."

The city was a bright carpet of twinkling lights when the *Red Rover* darted down out of a black sky, hovering for a moment over Trainor's Tower. When it flashed away, Bill was standing alone on top of the loftiest building on earth, in his pocket a sheaf of manuscript on which he had been at work for many hours, beside him a bulky package that contained the preserved body of the weird monster from Mars.

He opened the trapdoor—which was conveniently unlocked—took up the package, and clambered down a ladder into the observatory. An intent man was busy at the great telescope, which pointed toward the red planet Mars. The man looked understandingly at Bill, and nodded toward the elevator.

In half an hour Bill was exhibiting his package and his manuscript to the night editor of the *Herald-Sun*.

"The greatest news in the century!" he cried. "The Earth attacked by Mars! It was a Martian ship that took the *Helicon*. I have one of the dead creatures from Mars in this box."

The astounded editor formed a quick opinion that his star reporter had met with some terrifying experience that had unsettled his brain. He listened skeptically while Bill related a true enough account of the cruise of the Moon Patrol ships, and of the battle with the blue globe. Bill omitted any mention of the City of Space and its enigmatic ruler; but let it be assumed that the *Fury* had rammed the globe and that it had fallen in the desert. He ended with a wholly fictitious account of how a mysterious scientist had picked him up in a sunship, had told him of the invaders from Mars, and had sent him to collect two tons of vitalium to equip his ship for a raid on Mars. Bill had spent many hours in planning his story; he was sure that it sounded as plausible as the amazing reality of the Prince of Space and his wonderful city.

The skeptical editor was finally convinced, as much by his faith in Bill's probity as by the body of the green monster, the scraps of a strange white metal, and the photographs, which he presented as material evidence. The editor radioed to have a plane sent from El Paso, Texas, to investigate the wrecks. When it was reported that they were just as Bill had said, the *Herald-Sun* issued an extra, which carried Bill's full account, with photographs of the dead monster, and scientific accounts of the other evidence. There was an appeal for two tons of vitalium, to enable the unknown scientist to save the world by making a raid on Mars.

The story created an enormous sensation all over the world. A good many people believed it. The *Herald-Sun* actually received half a million eagles in subscriptions to buy the vitalium—a sum sufficient to purchase about eleven ounces of that precious metal.

Most of the world laughed. It was charged that Bill was insane. It was charged that the *Herald-Sun* was attempting to expand its circulation by a baseless canard. Worse, it was charged that Bill, perhaps in complicity with the management of the great newspaper, was making the discovery of a new sort of creature in some far corner of the world the basis for a gigantic fraud, to secure that vast amount of vitalium.

Examination proved that the wrecks in the desert had been demolished by explosion instead of by falling. A court injunction was filed against the *Herald-Sun* to prevent collection of the subscriptions, and Bill might have been arrested, if he had not wisely retired to Trainor's Tower.

Finally, it was charged that the pirate, the Prince of Space, was at the bottom of it—possibly the charge was suggested by the fact that the chief object of the Prince's raids had always been vitalium. A rival paper asserted that the pirate must have captured Bill and sent him back to Earth with this fraud.

Public excitement became so great that the reward for the capture of Prince of Space, dead or alive, was raised from ten to fifteen million eagles.

Twenty-four hours later after he had been landed on Trainor's Tower, Bill was waiting there again, with bright stars above him, and the carpet of fire that was New York spread in great squares beneath him. The slim silver ship came gliding down, and hung just beside the vitrolite dome while eager hands helped him through the air lock. Beyond, he found the Prince waiting, with a question in his eyes.

"No luck," Bill grunted hopelessly. "Nobody believed it. And the town was getting too hot for me. Lucky I had a getaway."

The Prince smiled bitterly as the newspaperman told of his attempt to enlist the aid of humanity.

"About what I expected," he said. "Men will act like men. It might be better, in the history of the cosmos, to let the Martians have this old world. They might make something better of it. But I am going to give humanity a chance—if I can. Perhaps man will develop into something better, in a million years."

"Then there is still a chance—without the vitalium?" Bill asked eagerly.

"Not without vitalium. We have to go to Mars. We must have the metal to fit our flier for the trip. But I have needed vitalium before; when I could not buy it. I took it."

"You mean—piracy!" Bill gasped.

"Am I not the Prince of Space—'notorious interplanetary outlaw' as you have termed me in your paper? And is not the good of the many more than the good of the few? May I not take a few pounds of metal from a rich corporation, to save the earth for humanity?"

"I told you to count me in," said Bill. "The idea was just a little revolutionary."

"We haven't wasted any time while you were in New York. I have means of keeping posted on the shipments of vitalium from the moon. We have found that the sunship *Triton* leaves the moon in about twenty hours, with three months production of the vitalium mines in the Kepler crater. It should be well over two tons."

Thirty hours later the *Red Rover* was drifting at rest in the lunar lane, with ray tubes dead and no light showing. Men at her telescopes scanned the heavens moonward for sight of the white repulsion rays of the *Triton* and her convoy.

Bill was with Captain Brand in the bridge-room. Eager light flashed in Brand's eyes as he peered through the telescopes, watched his instruments, and spoke brisk orders into the tube.

"How does it feel to be a pirate," Bill asked, "after so many years spent hunting them down?"

Captain Brand grinned. "You know," he said, "I've wanted to be a buccaneer ever since I was about four years old. I couldn't, of course, so I took the next best thing, and hunted them. I'm not exactly grieving my heart out over what has happened. But I feel sorry for my old pals of the Moon Patrol. Somebody is going to get hurt."

"And it may be we," said Bill. "The *Triton* will be convoyed by several war-fliers, and she can fight with her own rays. It looks to me like a hard nut to crack."

"I used to dream about how I would take a ship if I were the Prince of Space," said Captain Brand. "I've just been talking our course of action over with him. We've agreed on a plan."

In an hour the Prince and Dr. Trainor entered the bridge. Paula appeared in a few moments. Her face was drawn and pale; unhappiness cast a shadow in her brown eyes. Eagerly, she asked the Prince how he was feeling.

"Oh, about as well as ever, thanks," the lean young man replied in a careless voice. His dark, enigmatic eyes fell upon her face. He must have noticed her pallor and evident unhappiness. He met her eyes for a moment, then took a quick step toward her. Bill saw a great tenderness almost breaking past the bitter cynicism in those dark eyes. Then the Prince checked himself, spoke shortly:

"We are preparing for action, Paula. Perhaps you should go back to your stateroom until it is over."

The girl turned silently and moved out of the room. Bill thought she would have tottered and fallen if there had been enough gravity or acceleration to make one fall.

In a few minutes a little group of flickering lights appeared among the stars ahead, just beside the huge, crater-scarred, golden disk of the moon.

"The *Triton* and her convoy!" shouted the men at the telescopes.

"All men to their stations, and clear the ship for action!" Captain Brand gave the order.

"Two Moon Patrol sunships are ahead, cruising fifty miles apart," came the word from the telescope. "A hundred miles behind them is the *Triton,* with two more Patrol fliers twenty-five miles behind her and fifty miles apart."

Brand spoke to the Prince, who nodded. And Brand gave the order.

"Show no lights. Work the ship around with the gyroscopes until our rear battery of tubes will cover the right Patrol ship of the leading pair, and our bow tubes the other."

The whir of the electric motors came from below. The fliers swung about, hanging still in the path of the approaching *Triton*.

"All ready, sir," came a voice from the tube.

A few anxious minutes went by. Then the *Red Rover,* dark and silent, was hanging squarely between the two forward Patrol ships, about twenty-five miles from each of them.

"Fire constantly with all tubes, fore and aft, until the enemy appears to be disabled," Brand gave the order. The Prince spoke to him, and he added, "Inflict no unnecessary damage."

Dazzling white rays flashed from the tubes. Swiftly, they found the two forward sunships. The slender octagons of silver shone white under the rays. They reeled, whirled about, end over end, under the terrific pressure of atomic bombardment. In a moment they glowed with dull red incandescence, swiftly became white. A bluish haze spread about them—the discharge of the electric energy carried by the atoms, which would electrocute any man not insulated against it.

From the three other ships flaming white rays darted, searching for the *Red Rover.* But they had hardly found the mark when Brand ordered his rays snapped out. The two vessels he had struck were but whirling masses of incandescent wreckage—completely out of the battle, though most of the men aboard them still survived in their insulated cells.

The Prince himself spoke into the tube. "Maneuver number forty-one. Drive for the *Triton.*"

Driven by alternate burst from front and rear motor tubes, the *Red Rover* started a curiously irregular course toward the treasure ship. Spinning end over end, describing irregular curves, she must have been an almost impossible target.

And twice during each spin, when her axis was in line with the *Triton,* all tubes were fired for an instant, striking the treasure ship with a force that reeled and staggered her, leaving her plates half-fused, twisted and broken.

Three times a ray caught the *Red Rover* for an instant, but her amazing maneuvers, which had evidently been long practiced by her crew, carried her on a course so erratic and puzzling that the few rays that found her were soon shaken off.

Before the pirate flier reached the *Triton,* the treasure vessel was drifting helpless, with all rays out. The *Red Rover* passed by her, continuing on her dizzily whirling course until she was directly between the two remaining fliers.

"Hold her still," the Prince then shouted into the tube. "And fire all rays, fore and aft."

Blinding opalescent rays jetted viciously from the two rings of tubes. Since the *Red Rover* lay between the two vessels, they could not avoid firing upon each other. Her own rays, being fired in opposite directions, served to balance each other and hold her at rest, while the rays of the enemy, as well as those of the pirate that impinged upon them, tended to send them into spinning flight through space.

Blinding fluorescence obscured the vitrolite panels, and the stout walls of the *Red Rover* groaned beneath the pressure of the hail of atoms upon them. Swiftly they would heat, soften, collapse. Or the insulation would burn away and the electric charge electrocute her passengers.

The enemy was in a state as bad. The white beams of the pirate flier had found them earlier, and could be held upon them more efficiently. It was a contest of endurance.

Suddenly the jets of opalescence snapped off the pirate. Bill gazing out into star-dusted space, saw the two Patrol vessels spinning in mad flight before the pressure of the rays, glowing white in incandescent twisted ruin.

A few minutes later the *Red Rover* was drifting beside the *Triton* holding the wrecked treasure-flier with electromagnetic plates. The air lock of the pirate vessel opened to release a dozen men in metal vacuum suits, armed with ray pistols and equipped with wrecking tools and oxygen lances. The Prince was their leader.

They forced the air lock of the *Triton,* and entered the wreck. In a few minutes grotesque metal-suited figures appeared again, carrying heavy leaden tubes filled with the precious vitalium.

The *Red Rover* was speeding into space, an hour later, under full power. The Prince of Space was in the bridge room, with Bill, Captain Brand, Dr. Trainor, and Paula. Bill noticed that the girl seemed pathetically joyous at the Prince's safety, though he gave her scant attention.

"We have the two tons of vitalium," said the Prince. "Nearly forty-six hundred pounds, in fact. Easily enough to furnish power for the voyage to Mars. We have the metal— provided we can get away with it."

"Is there still danger?" Paula inquired nervously.

"Yes. Most of the passengers of the *Triton* were still alive. When I gave her captain my card, he told me that they sent a heliographic S.O.S. as soon as we attacked. Some forty or fifty fliers of the Moon Patrol will be hot on our trail."

The *Red Rover* flew on into space, under all her power. Presently the lookouts picked up a score of tiny flickering points of light behind them. The Moon Patrol was in hot pursuit.

"Old friends of mine," said Captain Brand. "Everyone of them would give his life to see us caught. And I suppose everyone of them feels now that he has a slice of that fifteen million eagles reward. The Moon Patrol never gives up and never admits defeat."

Tense, anxious hours went by while every battery was delivering its maximum current, and every motor tube was operating at its absolutely highest potential.

Paula waited on the bridge, anxiously solicitous for the Prince's health—he was still pale and weak from the adventure in the desert. Presently, evidently noticing how tired and worried she looked, he sent her to her stateroom to rest. She went, in tears.

"No chance to fight, if they run us down," said Captain Brand. "We can handle four, but not forty."

Time dragged heavily. The *Red Rover* flew out into space, past the moon, on such a course as would not draw pursuit toward the City of Space. Her maximum acceleration was slightly greater than that of the Moon Patrol fliers, because of the greater number and power of her motor tubes. Steadily she forged away from her pursuers.

At last the flickering lights behind could be seen no longer.

But the *Red Rover* continued in a straight line, at the top of her speed, for many hours, before she turned and slipped cautiously toward the secret City of Space. She reached it in safety, was let through the air lock. Once more Bill looked out upon the amazing city upon the inner wall of a spinning cylinder. He enjoyed the remarkable experience of a walk along a street three miles in length, which brought him up in an unbroken curve, and back to where he had started.

It took a week to refit the *Red Rover*, in preparation for the voyage to Mars. Her motor ray tubes were rebuilt, and additional vitalium generators installed. The precious metal taken from the *Triton* was built into new batteries to supply power for the long voyage. Good stocks of food, water, and compressed oxygen were taken aboard, as well as weapons and scientific equipment of all variety.

"We start for Mars in thirty minutes," Captain Brand told Bill when the warning gong had called him and the others aboard.

CHAPTER SIX
The Red Star of War

The *Red Rover* slipped out through the great air lock of the City of Space, and put her bow toward Mars. The star of the war-god hung before her in the silver-dusted darkness of the faint constellation of Capricornus, a tiny brilliant disk of ocherous red. The Prince of Space, outlawed by the world of his birth, was hurtling out through space in a mad attempt to save that world from the horrors of Martian invasion.

The red point that was Mars hung almost above them, it seemed, almost in the center of the vitrolite dome of the bridge. "We are not heading directly for the planet," Captain Brand told Bill. "Its orbital velocity must be considered. We are moving toward the point that it will occupy in twenty days."

"We can make it in twenty days? Three million miles a day?"

"Easily, if the vitalium holds out, and if we don't collide with a meteorite. There is no limit to speed in space, certainly no practical limit. Acceleration is the important question."

"We may collide with a meteorite you say? Is there much danger?"

"A good deal. The meteorites travel in swarms, which follow regular orbits about the sun. We have accurate charts of the swarms whose orbits cross those of the earth and moon. Now we are entering unexplored territory. And most of them are so small, of course, that no telescope would reveal them in time. Merely little pebbles, moving with a speed about a dozen times that of a bullet from an old-fashioned rifle."

"And what are we going to do if we live to get to Mars?"

"A big question," Brand grinned. "We could hardly mop up a whole planet with the motor rays. Trainor has a few of his rocket torpedoes, but not enough to make much impression upon a belligerent planet. The Prince and Trainor have a laboratory rigged up down below. They are doing a lot of work. A new weapon, I understand. I don't know what will come of it."

Presently Bill found his way down the ladder to the laboratory. He found the Prince of Space and Dr. Trainor hard at work. He learned little by watching them, save that they were experimenting upon small animals, green plants, and samples of the rare vitalium. High tension electricity, electron tubes, and various rays seemed to be in use.

Noticing his interest, the Prince said, "You know that vitalium was first discovered in vitamins, in infinitesimal quantities. The metal seems to be at the basis of all life. It is the trace of vitalium in chlorophyll that enables the green leaves of plants to utilize the energy of sunlight. We are trying to determine the nature of the essential force of life—we know that the question is bound up with the radioactivity of vitalium. We have made a good deal of progress, and complete success would give us a powerful instrumentality."

Paula was working with them in the laboratory, making a capable and eager assistant—she had been her father's helper since her girlhood. Bill noticed that she seemed happy only when near the Prince, that the weight of unhappiness and trouble left her brown eyes only when she was able to help him with some task, or when her skill brought a word or glance of approval from him.

The Prince himself seemed entirely absorbed in his work; he treated the girl courteously enough, but seemed altogether impersonal toward her. To him, she seemed only to be a fellow scientist. Yet Bill knew that the Prince was aware of the girl's feelings—and he suspected that the Prince was trying to stifle a growing reciprocal emotion of his own.

Bill spent long hours on the bridge with Captain Brand, staring out at the star-scattered midnight of space. The earth shrank quickly, until it was a tiny green disk, with the moon an almost invisible white speck beside it. Day by day, Mars grew larger. It swelled from an ocher point to a little red disk.

Often Bill scanned the spinning scarlet globe through a telescope. He could see the white polar caps, the dark equatorial regions, the black lines of the canals. And after many days, he could see the little blue circle that had been visible in the giant telescope on Trainor's Tower.

"It must be something enormous, to stand out so plainly," he said when he showed it to Captain Brand.

"I suppose so. Even now, we could see nothing with a diameter of less than a mile or so."

"If it's a ship, it must be darned big—big enough for the whole race of 'em to get aboard."

Bill was standing, a few hours later, gazing out through the vitrolite panels at the red-winged splendor of the sun, when suddenly he heard a series of terrific crashes. The ship rocked and trembled beneath him; he heard the reverberation of hammered metal, and the hiss of escaping air.

"Meteorite!" screamed Brand.

Wildly, he pointed to the vitrolite dome above. In three places the heavy crystal was shattered, a little hole drilled through it, surrounded with radiating cracks. In two other sections the heavy metal wall was dented. Through the holes, the air was hissing out. It formed a white cloud outside, and glistening frost gathered quickly on the crystal panels.

Bill felt the air suddenly drawn from his lungs. He gasped for breath. The bridge was abruptly cold. Little particles of snow danced across it.

"The air is going," Brand gasped. "We'll suffocate."

He touched a lever and a heavy cover fell across the ladder shaft, locked itself, making the floor an airtight bulkhead.

"That's right," Bill tried to say. "Give others—chance."

His voice had failed. A soaring came in his ears. He felt as if a malignant giant were sucking out his breath. The room grew dark, swam about him. He reeled; he was blind. A sudden chill came over his limbs—the infinite cold of space. He felt hot blood spurting from his nose, freezing on his face. Faintly he heard Brand moving, as he staggered and fell into unconsciousness.

When he looked about again, air and warmth were coming back. He saw that the shaft was still sealed, but air was hissing into the room through a valve. Captain Brand lay inert beside him on the floor. He looked up at the dome, saw that soft rubber patches had been placed over the holes, where air-pressure held them fast. The Captain had saved the ship before he fell.

In a moment the door opened. Dr. Trainor rushed in, with Prince and others behind him. They picked up the unconscious Brand and rushed him down to the infirmary. The plucky captain had been almost asphyxiated, but administration of pure oxygen restored him to consciousness. On the following day he was back on the bridge.

The *Red Rover* had been eighteen days out from the City of Space. The loss of air due to collision with the meteorites had brought inconveniences, but good progress had been made. It was only two more days to Mars. The forward tubes had been going many hours, to retard the ship.

"Object dead ahead!" called a lookout from his telescope.

"A small blue globe, coming directly toward us," he added, a moment later.

"Another of their ships, setting out for the earth," Brand muttered. "It will about cook our goose…"

In a few moments the Prince and Dr. Trainor had rushed up the ladder from the laboratory. The blue globe was rushing swiftly toward them; and the *Red Rover* was plunging forward at many thousand miles per hour.

"We can't run from it," said Brand. "It is still fifty thousand miles away, but we are going far too fast to stop in that distance. We will pass it in about five minutes."

"If we can't stop, we go ahead," the Prince said, smiling grimly.

"We might try a torpedo on 'em," suggested Dr. Trainor. He had mounted a tube to fire his rocket torpedoes from the bridge. "It will have all the speed its own motor rays can develop, plus what the ship has at present, plus the relative velocity of the globe. That might carry it through."

The Prince nodded assent.

Trainor slipped a slender, gleaming rocket into his tube, sighted it, moved the lever that set the projectile to spinning, and fired. The little white flame of the motor rays dwindled and vanished ahead of them. Quickly, Trainor fired again, and then a third time.

"Switch off the rays and darken the lights," the Prince ordered. "With combined speeds of ten thousand miles a minute, we might pass them without being seen—if they haven't sighted us already."

For long seconds they hurtled onward in tense silence. Bill was at a telescope. Against the silver and black background of space, the little blue disk of the Martian ship was growing swiftly.

Suddenly a bright purple spark appeared against the blue, grew swiftly brighter.

"An atomic bomb!" he cried. "They saw us. We are lost!"

He tensed himself, waiting for the purple flash that would mean the end. But the words were hardly out of his mouth when he saw a tiny sheet of violet flame far ahead of them. It flared up suddenly, and vanished as abruptly. The blue disk of the ship still hung before them, but the purple spark was gone. For a moment he was puzzled. Then he understood.

"The atomic bomb struck a torpedo!" he shouted. "Its exploded. And if they think it was we—"

"Perhaps they can't see us, with the rays out," Brand said.

"It is unlikely," Trainor observed, "that the bomb actually struck one of our torpedoes. More likely it was set to be detonated by the gravitational attraction of any object that passed near it."

Still watching the azure globe, Bill saw a sudden flare of orange light against it. A great burst of yellow flame. The blue ball crumpled behind the flame. The orange went out, and the blue vanished with it. Only twisted scraps of white metal were left.

"The second torpedo struck the Martian!" Bill cried.

"And you notice that the blue went out," said Dr. Trainor. "It must be merely a vibratory screen."

The *Red Rover* hurtled on through space, toward the crimson planet that hour by hour and minute by minute expanded before her. The blue disk was now plainly visible against the red. It was apparently a huge globe of azure, similar to the ships they had met, but at least a mile in diameter. She lay just off the red desert, near an important junction of "canals."

"Some huge machine, screened by the blue wall of vibration," Dr. Trainor suggested.

During the last two days the Prince and Dr. Trainor, and their eager assistant, Paula, had worked steadily in the laboratory, without pause for rest. Bill was with them when the Prince threw down his pencil and announced the result of his last calculation.

"The problem is solved," he said. "And its answer means both success and failure. We have mastered the secret of life. We have unlocked the mystery of the ages! A terrific force is at our command—a force great enough to sweep man to the millennium, or to wipe out a planet! But that force is useless without the apparatus to release it."

"We have the laboratory—" Trainor began.

"But we lack one essential thing. We must have a small amount of cerium, one of the rare earth metals. For the electrode, you know, inside the vitalium grid in our new vacuum tube. And there is not a gram of cerium in all our supplies."

"We can go back to the Earth—" said Trainor.

"That will mean forty days gone, before we could come back—more than forty, because we would have to stop at the City of Space to refit. And all the perils of the meteorites again. I am sure that in less than forty days the Martians will be putting the machine in that enormous blue globe to its dreadful use."

"Then we must land on Mars and find the metal," said Captain Brand, who had been listening by the door.

"Exactly," said the Prince. "You will pick out a spot that looks deserted, at a great distance from the blue globe. Somewhere in the mountains, as far back as possible from the canals. Land there just after midnight. We will have mining and prospecting equipment ready to go to work when day comes. Almost any sort of ore ought to yield the small quantity of cerium we need."

"Very good, sir," said Brand.

A few hours later the *Red Rover* was sweeping around Mars, on a long curve, many thousands of miles from the surface of the red planet.

"We'll pick out the spot to land while the sun is shinning on it," Captain Brand told Bill. "Then we can keep over it, as it sweeps around into the shadow, timing ourselves to land just after midnight."

"Isn't there danger that we may be seen?"

"Of course. We can only minimize it by keeping a few thousand miles above the surface as long as it is day, and landing at night, and in a deserted section."

As they drew nearer, the telescope revealed the surface of the hostile planet more distinctly. Bill peered intently into an eyepiece, scanning the red globe for signs of its malignant inhabitants.

"The canals seem to be strips of greenish vegetation, irrigated from some sort of irrigation system that brings water from the melting ice-caps," he said.

"Lowell, the old American astronomer, knew that two hundred years ago," said Captain Brand, "though some of his contemporaries claimed that they could not see the 'canals.'"

"I can make out low green trees, and metal structures. I think there are long pipes, as well as open channels, to spread the water. And I see a great dome of white metal—it must be five hundred feet across. There are several of them in sight, mostly located where the canals intersect."

"They might be great community buildings—cities," suggested Brand. "On account of the dust-storms that so often hide the surface of the planet, it would probably be necessary to cover a city up in some way."

"And I see something moving. A little blue dot, it seems. Probably a little flier on the same order as those we have seen; but only a few feet in diameter. It seemed to be sailing from one of the white domes to another."

Brand moved to another telescope.

"Yes, I see them. Two in one place. They seem to be floating along, high and fast. And just to the right is a whole line of them, flying one behind the other. Crossing a patch of red desert."

"What's this?" Bill cried in some excitement. "Looks like animals of some kind in a pen. They look like people, almost."

"What? Let me see…"

Brand rushed over from his telescope. Bill relinquished him the instrument. "See? Just above the center of the field. Right in the edge of that cultivated strip, by what looks like a big aluminum water-pipe."

"Yes. Yes, I see something. A big stockade. And it has things in it. But not men, I think. They are gray and hairy. But they seem to walk on two legs."

"Something like apes, maybe."

"I've got it," cried Brand. "They're domestic animals! The ruling Martians are parasites. They must have something to suck blood out of. They live on these creatures!"

"Probably so," Bill admitted. "Do you suppose they will keep people penned up that way, if they conquer the world?"

"Likely." He shuddered. "No good in thinking of it. We must be selecting the place to land."

He returned to his instrument.

"I've got it," he said presently. "A low mountain, in a big sweep of red desert. About sixty degrees north of the equator. Not a canal or a white dome in a hundred miles."

Long hours went by, while the *Red Rover* hung above the chosen landing place, waiting for it to sweep into the shadow of night. Bill peered intently through his telescope, watching the narrow strips of vegetation across the bare stretches of orange desert. He studied the bright metal and gray masonry of irrigation works, the widely scattered, white metal domes that seemed to cover cities, the hurtling blue globes that flashed in swift flight between them. Two or three time; he caught sight of a tiny, creeping green thing that he thought was one of the hideous, blood-sucking Martians. And he saw half a dozen broad metal pens, or pastures, in which the hairy gray bipeds were confined.

Shining machines were moving across the green strips of fertile land, evidently cultivating them.

The Prince, Dr. Trainor, and Paula were asleep in their staterooms. Bill retired for a short rest, came back to find the planet beneath them in darkness. The *Red Rover* was dropping swiftly, with Captain Brand still at the bridge,

Rapidly, the stars vanished in an expanding circle below them. Phobos and Deimos, the small moons of Mars, hurtling across the sky with different velocities shed scant light upon the barren desert below. Captain Brand eased the ship down, using the rays as little as possible, to cut down the danger of detection.

The *Red Rover* dropped silently to the center of a low cliff-rimmed plateau that rose from the red, sandy desert. In the faint light of star; and hurtling moons, the ocherous waste lay flat in all directions—there are no high mountains on Mars. The air was clear, and so thin that the stars shone with hot brilliance, almost, Bill thought, as if the ship were still out in space.

Silent hours went by, as they waited for dawn. The thin white disk of the nearer moon slid down beneath the black eastern horizon, and rose again to make another hurtling flight.

Just before dawn the Prince appeared, an eager smile on his alert lean face, evidently well recovered from the long struggling in the laboratory.

"I've all the mining machinery ready," Captain Brand told him. "We can get out as soon as it's warm enough—it's a hundred and fifty below zero out there now."

"It ought to warm up right soon after sunrise—thin as this air is. You seem to have picked about the loneliest spot on the planet, all right. There's a lot of danger, though, that we may be discovered before we get the cerium."

"Funny feeling to be the first men on a new world," said Bill.

"But we're not the first," the Prince said. "I am sure that Envers landed on Mars—I think the Martian ships are based on a study of his machinery."

"Envers may have waited here in the desert for the sun to rise, just as we are doing," murmured Brand. "In fact, if he wanted to look around without being seen, he may have landed right near here. This is probably the best place on the planet to land without being detected."

CHAPTER SEVEN
A Mine on Mars

The sun came up small and white and hot, shining from a black sky upon an endless level orange waste of rocks and sand, broken with a black swamp in the distant north. Even from the eminence of the time-worn plateau, the straight horizon seemed far nearer than on earth, due to the greater curvature of the planet's surface.

Men were gathering about the air lock, under the direction of the Prince, assembling mining equipment.

"Shall we be able to go out without vacuum suits?" Bill asked Captain Brand.

"I think so, when it gets warm enough. The air is light—the amount of oxygen at the surface is about equal to that in the air nine miles above sea level on earth. But the pull of gravity here is only about one-third as much as it is on the earth, and less oxygen will be required to furnish energy. I think we can stand it, if we don't take too much exertion."

The rays of the oddly small sun beat fiercely through the thin air. Soon the Prince went into the air lock, closed the inner door behind him and started the pumps. When the dial showed the pressures equalized he opened the outer door, and stepped out upon the red rocks.

All were watching him intently, through the vitrolite panels. Paula clasped her hands in nervous anxiety. Bill saw the Prince step confidently out, sniff the air as though testing it, and take a few deep breaths. Then he drew his legs beneath him and made an astounding leap that carried him twenty feet high. He fell in a long arc, struck on his shoulder in a pile of loose red sand. He got up, gasping for air as if the effort had exhausted him, and staggered back to the air lock. Quickly he sealed the outer door behind him, opened the valve, and raised the pressure.

"Feels funny," he said when he opened the inner door. "Like trying to breathe on top of a mountain—only more so. The jump was great fun, but rather exhausting. I imagine it would be dangerous for a fellow with a weak heart. All right to come out now. Air is still cool, but the rocks are getting hot under the sun."

He held open the door. "The guards will come first."

Six of the thirty-odd members of the crew had been detailed to act as guards, to prevent surprise. Each was to carry two rocket torpedoes—such a burden was not too much upon this planet, with its lesser gravity. They would watch from the cliffs at the edge of the little plateau upon which the sunship had landed.

Bill and four other men entered the air lock—and Paula. The girl had insisted upon having some duty assigned to her, and this had seemed easier than the mining.

The door was closed behind them, the air pumped out until Bill gasped for breath and heard a drumming in his ears. Then the outer door was opened and they looked out upon Mars. Motion was easy, yet the slightest effort was tiring. Bill found himself panting merely from the exertion of lifting the two heavy torpedoes to his shoulders.

With Paula behind him, he stepped through the outer door. The air felt chill and thin. Loose red sand crumbled yieldingly under their feet.

They separated at the door, Bill starting toward the south end of the plateau, Paula toward the north point, and the men going to stations along the sides.

"Just lie at the top of the cliffs and watch," the Prince had ordered. "When you have anything to report, flash with your ray pistols, in code. Signal every thirty minutes, anyhow. We will have a man watching from the bridge. Report to him anything moving. We will fire off a red signal rocket when you are to come back."

He had tried to keep Paula from going out, but the girl had insisted. At last he had agreed.

"Better to have you keeping watch than handling a pick and shovel, or pushing a barrow," he had told her. "But I hate to see you go so far off. Something might happen. If they find us, though, they will probably get us all. Don't get hurt."

Bill had seen the Prince looking anxiously at the slender, brown-eyed girl as they entered the air lock. He had seen him move forward quickly, as though to ask her to come back— move forward, and then turn aside with a flush that became a bitterly cynical smile.

As Bill walked across the top of the barren red plateau, he looked back at the girl moving slowly in the opposite direction. He had glanced at her eyes as they left the ship. They were shadowed, heavy-lidded. In their brown depths lurked despair and tragic determination. Bill, watching her now, thought that all life had gone out of her. She seemed a dull automaton, driven only by the energy of a determined will. All hope and life and vivacity had gone from her manner. Yet she walked as if she had a stern task to do.

"I wonder—" Bill muttered. "Can she mean—suicide?"

He turned uncertainly, as if to go after her. Then, deciding that his thought was mere fancy, he trudged on across the red plateau to his station.

Behind him, he saw other parties emerging from the air lock. The Prince and Dr. Trainor were setting up apparatus of some kind, probably, Bill thought, to take magnetic and meteorological observations. Men with prospecting hammers were scattering over all the plateau.

"Almost any sort of ferruginous rock is sure to contain the tiny amount of cerium we need," Dr. Trainor had said.

Bill reached the end of the plateau. The age-worn cliffs of red granite and burned lava fell sheer for a hundred feet, to a long slope of talus. Below the rubble of sand and boulders the flat desert stretched away, almost visibly curving to vanish beneath the near red horizon.

It was a desolate and depressing scene, this view of a dead and sun-baked planet. There was no sign of living thing, no moving object, no green of life—the canals, with their verdure, were far out of sight.

"Hard to realize there's a race of vampires across there, living in great metal domes," Bill muttered, as he threw himself flat on the rocks at the lip of the precipice, and leveled one of the heavy torpedoes before him. "But I don't blame 'em for wanting to go to a more cheerful world."

Looking behind him, he soon saw men busy with electric drills not a hundred yards from the slender silver cylinder that was the *Red Rover.* The earth quivered beneath him as a shot was set off, and he saw a great fountain of crushed rock thrown into the air.

Men with barrows, an hour later, were wheeling the crushed rock to gleaming electrical reducing apparatus that Dr. Trainor and the Prince were setting up beside the sunship. Evidently there had been no difficulty in finding ore that carried a satisfactory amount of cerium.

Bill continued to scan the orange-red desert below him through the powerful telescope along the rocket tube. He kept his watch before him, and at half-hour intervals sent the three short flashes with his ray pistol, which meant "All is well."

Two hours must have gone by before he saw the blue globe. It came into view low over the red rim of the desert below him, crept closer on a wavering path.

"Martian ship in view," he signaled. "A blue globe, about ten feet in diameter. Follows curious winding course, as if following something."

"Keep rocket trained upon it," came the cautiously flashed reply. "Fire if it observes us."

"Globe following animals," he flashed back. "Two grayish bipeds leaping before it. Running with marvelous agility."

He was peering through the telescope sight of the rocket tube. Keeping the cross hairs upon the little blue globe, he could still see the creatures that fled before it. They were almost like men—or erect, hairy apes. Bipeds, they were, with human-like arms, and erect heads. Covered with short gray hair or fur, they carried no weapons.

They fled from the globe at a curious leaping run, which carried them over the flat red desert with remarkable speed. They came straight for the foot of the cliff from which Bill watched, the blue globe close behind them. When one of them stumbled over a block of lava and fell sprawling headlong on the sand, the other gray creature stopped to help it. The blue globe stopped, too, hanging still twenty feet above the red sand, waited for them to rise and run desperately on again.

Bill felt a quick flood of sympathy for the gray creatures. One had stopped to help the other. That meant that they felt affection. And the globe had waited for them to run again. It seemed to be baiting them maliciously. Almost he fired the rocket. But his orders had been not to fire unless the ship were discovered.

Now they were not a mile away. Suddenly Bill perceived a tiny, light-gray object grasped close to the breast of one of the gray bipeds. Evidently it was a young one, in the arms of its mother. The other creature seemed a male. It was the mother that had fallen.

They came on toward the cliff.

They were very clearly in view, and not five hundred yards below, when the female fell again. The male stopped to aid her, and the globe poised itself above them, waited. The mother seemed unable to rise. The other creature lifted her, and she fell limply back.

As if in rage, the gray male sprang toward the blue globe, crouching.

A tiny purple spark leapt from it. A flash of violet fire enveloped him. He was flung twisted and sprawling to the ground. Burned and torn and bleeding, he drew himself to all fours, and crept on toward the blue globe.

Suddenly the sphere dropped to the ground. A round panel swung open in its side—it was turned from Bill so that he could not see within. Green things crept out. They were creatures like the one he had seen in the Mexican desert—a cluster of slender, flexible green tentacles, with suction disks, an insignificant green body, and three malevolent purple eyes, at the ends of foot-long stalks.

There were three of the things.

The creeping male flung himself madly upon one of them. It coiled itself about him; suction disks fastened themselves against his skin. For a time he writhed and struggled, fighting in agony against the squeezing green coils. Then he was still.

One of the things grasped the little gray object in the mother's arms. She fought to shield it, to cover it with her own body. It was torn away from her, hidden in the hideously writhing green coils.

The third of the monsters flung itself upon the mother, wrapping snake-like tentacles about her, dragging her struggling body down shuddering and writhing in agony while the blood of life was sucked from it.

Bill watched, silent and trembling with horror.

"The things chased them—*for fun*," he muttered fiercely. "Just a sample of what it will be on the earth—if we don't stop 'em."

Presently the green monsters left their victims—which were now mere shriveled husks. They dragged themselves back into the blue globe, which rose swiftly into the air. The round panel had closed.

From his station on the cliff, Bill watched the thing through the telescope sight of the rocket, keeping the cross hairs upon it. It came up to his own level—above it. Suddenly it paused. He was sure that the things in it had seen the *Red Rover*.

Quickly, he pressed a little nickeled lever. A soft whir came from the rocket tube. He pressed the red button. The torpedo leapt forward, with the white rays driving back. The empty shell was flung back in Bill's hand.

A great burst of vivid orange flame enveloped the cobalt globe. It disintegrated into a rain of white metal fragments.

"Take that, damn you," he muttered in fierce satisfaction.

"Globe brought down successfully," he flashed. "Evidently it had sighted us. Green Martians from it had killed gray bipeds. May I inspect remains?"

"You may," permission was flashed back from the Prince. "But be absent not over half an hour."

In a moment another message came. "All lookouts be doubly alert. Globe may be searched for. Miners making good progress. We can leave by sunset. Courage! –The Prince."

Strapping the remaining rocket torpedo to his shoulders, and thrusting his ray pistol ready in his belt, Bill walked back along the brink of the precipice until he saw a comparatively easy way to the red plain below, and scrambled over the rim. Erosion of untold ages had left cracks and irregularities in the rock. Because of the slighter gravity of Mars, it was a simple feat to support his weight with the grip of his fingers on a ledge. In five minutes he had clambered down to the bank of talus. Hurriedly he scrambled down over great fallen boulders, panting and gasping for breath in the thin air.

He reached the red sand of the plain—it was worn by winds of ages into an impalpable scarlet dust that rose in a thin, murky cloud about him, and settled in a blood-colored stain upon his perspiring limbs. The dry dust yielded beneath his feet as he made his way toward the silent gray bodies, making his progress most difficult.

Almost exhausted, he reached the gray creatures, examined them. They were far different from human beings, despite obvious similarities. Each of their "hands" had but three clawed digits; a curious, disk-like appendage took the place of the nose. In skeletal structure they were far different from *homo sapiens*.

Wearily Bill trudged back to the towering red cliff, red dust swirling up about him. He was oddly exhausted by his exertions, trifling as they had been. The murky red dust he inhaled was irritating to his nostrils; he choked and sneezed. Sweat ran in muddy red streams from his body, and he was suddenly very thirsty.

All the top of the red granite plateau—it was evidently the stone heart of an ancient mountain—was hidden from him. He could see nothing of the *Red Rover* or any of her crew. He could see no living thing.

The flat plain of red dust lay about him, curving below a near horizon. Loose dust sucked at his feet, rose about him in a suffocating saffron cloud. The sun, a little crimson globe in a blue-black sky, shone blisteringly. The sky was soberly dark, cold and hostile. In alarmed haste, he struggled toward the grim line of high, red cliffs.

Then he saw a round white object in the red sand.

Pausing to gasp for breath and to rub the sweat and red mud from his forehead, he kicked at it curiously. A sun-bleached human skull rolled out of the scarlet dust. He knew at once that it was human, not a skull of a creature like the gray things behind him on the sand.

With the unpleasant feeling that he was opening the forbidden book of some forgotten tragedy, he fell to his knees in the dust, and scooped about with his fingers. His right had closed upon a man's thigh bone. His left caught in a rotten leather belt, that pulled a human vertebra out of the dust. The belt had a tarnished silver buckle, and he looked at it with a gasp.

It bore an elaborate initial "E."

"E," he muttered. "Envers. He got to Mars. And died here. Trying to get to the mountain, I guess. Lord! What a death… A man all alone, in the dust and the sun. A strange world. Strange monsters."

The loneliness of the red desert, the mystery of it, and its alien spirit, wrapped itself about him like a mantle of fear. He staggered to his feet, and set off at a stumbling run through the sand toward the cliff. But in a moment he paused.

"He might have left something," he muttered.

He turned, and plodded back to where he had left the skull and the rotted belt, and dug again with his fingers. He found the rest of the skeleton, even bits of hair, clothing and human skin, preserved in the dry dust. He found an empty canteen, a rusty pocketknife, buttons, coins, and a ray pistol that was burned out.

Then his plowing fingers brought up a little black book from the dust.

It was Envers' diary.

Most of it was still legible. It is available in printed form today, and gives a detailed account of the tragic venture. The hopeful starting from earth. The dangers and discouragements of the voyage. A mutiny; half the crew killed. The thrill of landing on a new planet. The attack of the blue globes. How they took the ship, carried their prisoners to the pens, where they tried to use them to breed a new variety of domestic animals. Envers' escape, his desperate attempt to find the ship where they had landed in the desert.

Bill did not read it all then. He took time to read only that last tragic entry.

"Water all gone. See now I will never reach mountain where I landed. Probably they have moved sunship anyhow. Might have been better to have stayed in the pen. Food and water there... But how could God create such things? So hideous, so malignant! I pray they will not use my ship to go to earth. I hoped to find and destroy it. But it is too late."

Thick red dust swirled up in Bill's face. He tried to breathe, choked and sneezed and strangled. Looking up from the yellowed pages of the dead explorer's notebook, he saw great clouds of red dust hiding the darkly blue sky in the east.

It seemed almost that a colossal red-yellowed cylinder was being rolled swiftly upon him from eastward.

A dust-storm was upon him! One of the terrific dust storms of Mars, so fierce that they are visible to astronomers across forty million miles of space.

Clutching the faded notebook, he ran across the sand again, toward the red cliffs. The wind howled behind him, overtook him and came screaming about his ears. Red dust fogged chokingly about his head. The line of cliffs before him vanished in a murky red haze. The wind blew swiftly, yet it was thin, exerting little force. The dusty air became an acrid fluid, choking, unbreathable.

Blindly, he staggered on, toward the rocks. He reached them, fought his way up the bank of talus, scrambling over gigantic blocks of lava. The base of the cliff was before him, a massive, perpendicular wall, rising out of sight in red haze. He skirted it, saw a climbable chimney, scrambled up.

At last he drew himself over the top, and lay flat. Scarlet dust-clouds swirled about him; he could not see twenty yards. He made no attempt to find the *Red Rover;* he knew he could not locate it in the dust.

Hours passed as he lay there, blinded, suffocating, feeling the hot misery of acrid dust and perspiration caked in a drying mud upon his skin. Thin winds screamed about the rocks, hot as a furnace-blast. He leveled his torpedo, tried to watch. But he could see only a murky wall of red, with the sun biting through it like a tiny, round blood-ruby.

The red sun had been near the zenith. Slowly it crept down, toward an unseen horizon. It alone gave him an idea of direction, and of the passage of time. Then it, too, vanished in the dust.

Suddenly the wind was still. The dust settled slowly. In half an hour the red sun came into view again, just above the red western horizon. Objects about the mile-long plateau began to take shape. The *Red Rover* still lay where she had been, in the center. Men were still busily at work at the mining machinery—they had struggled on through the storm.

"All lookouts signal reports," the Prince flashed from the ship.

"Found Envers' body and brought his diary," Bill flashed when it came his turn.

"Now preparing to depart," came from the Prince. "Getting apparatus aboard. Have the required cerium. Return signal will be fired soon."

Bill watched the dusty sky, over whose formerly dark-blue face the storm had drawn a yellowish haze. In a few minutes he saw a blue globe. Then another, and a third. They were far toward the southeast, drifting high and fast through the saffron haze. It seemed that they were searching out the route over which the globe that he had brought down must have come.

"Three globe-ships in sight," he signaled. "Approaching us."

Some of the other lookouts had evidently seen them, for he saw the flicker of other ray pistols across the plateau.

Without preamble, the red signal rocket was fired. Bill heard the report of it—sharp and thin in the rare atmosphere. He saw the livid scarlet flare.

He got to his feet, shouldered the heavy rocket tube, and ran stumbling back to the *Red Rover*. He saw other men running; saw men struggling to get the mining machinery back on the ship.

Looking back, he saw the three blue globes swimming swiftly nearer. Then he saw others, a full score of them. They were far off, tiny circles of blue in the saffron sky. They seemed to be rapidly flying toward the *Red Rover*.

He looked expectantly northward, toward the end of the plateau to which Paula had gone. He saw nothing of her. She was not returning in answer to the signal rocket.

He was utterly exhausted when he reached the sunship, panting, gasping for the thin air. The others were all like himself, caked with dried red mud, gasping asthmatically from exertion and excitement. Men were struggling to get pieces of heavy machinery aboard the flier—vitalium power generators that had been used to heat the furnaces, and even a motor ray tube that had been borrowed from the ship's power plant for emergency use in the improvised smelter.

The Prince and Dr. Trainor were laboring furiously over an odd piece of apparatus. On the red sand beside the silver sunship, they had set up a tripod on which was mounted a curious glistening device. There were lenses, prisms, condensers, mirrors. The core of it seemed to be a strange vacuum tube, which had an electrode of cerium, surrounded with a queer vitalium grid. A tiny filament was glowing in it; and the induction coil which powered the tube, fed by vitalium batteries, was buzzing incessantly.

"Better get aboard, and off," Bill cried. "No use to lose our lives, our chance to save the world—just for a little mining machinery."

The Prince looked up in a moment, leaving the queer little device to Dr. Trainor. "Look at the Martian ships," he cried, sweeping out an arm. "Must be thirty in sight, swarming up like flies. We couldn't get away. And against those purple atomic bombs, the torpedoes wouldn't have a chance. Besides, we have some of the ship's machinery out here. Some generators, and a ray tube."

Bill looked up, saw the swarming blue globes, circling above them in the saffron sky, some of them not a mile above. He shrugged hopelessly, then looked anxiously off to the north again, scanning the red plateau.

"Paula. What's become of her?" he demanded.

"Paula? Is she gone?" The Prince turned from the tripod, looked around suddenly. "Paula! What could have happened to her?"

"A broken heart has happened to her," Bill told him.

"You think—you think—" stammered the Prince. There was sudden alarm in his dark eyes, and a great tender longing. His bitterly cynical smile was gone.

"Bill, she can't be gone!" he cried, almost in agony.

"You know she was on lookout duty at the north end of the plateau. She hasn't come back."

"I've got to find her!"

"What is it to you? I thought you didn't care," Bill was stern.

"I thought I didn't, except as a friend. But I was wrong. If she's gone, Bill—it will kill me!"

The Prince spun about with abrupt decision.

"Get everything aboard, and fit the ship to take off, as soon as possible," he ordered. "Dr. Trainor is in command. Give him any help he needs. Brand, test everything when the tube is replaced; keep the ship ready to fly." He turned swiftly to Trainor, who still worked deftly over the glittering little machine on the tripod. "Doc, you can operate that by yourself, as well as if I were here. Do your best—for mankind. I'm going to find your daughter."

Trainor nodded in silent assent, his fingers busy.

The Prince, sticking a ray pistol in his belt, set off at a desperate run toward the north end of the plateau. After a moment's hesitation, Bill staggered along behind him, still carrying the rocket torpedo strapped to his back.

It was only half a mile to the end of the plateau. In a few minutes the Prince was there. Bill staggered up just as he was reading a few scrawled words on a scrap of paper that he had found fastened to a boulder where Paula had been stationed.

"To the Prince of Space" it ran. "I can't go on. You must know that I love you—desperately. It was maddening to be with you, to know that you don't care. I know the story of your life, know that you can never care for me. The red dust is blowing now, and I am going down in the desert to die. Please don't look for me—it will do no good. Pardon me for writing this, but I wanted you to know—why I am going. Because I love you. Paula."

CHAPTER EIGHT
The Vitomaton

"I love Paula!" cried the Prince. "It happened all at once—when you said she was gone. Like a burst of light. Yet it must have been growing for weeks. It was getting so I couldn't work in the lab, unless she was there. God! It must have been hard for her. I was fighting it; I tried to hide what I was beginning to feel, tried to treat her as if she were a man. Now—she's *gone.*"

Bill looked back to the *Red Rover,* half a mile behind them. She lay still, burnished silver cylinder on the red sand. He could see Trainor beside her, still working over the curious little device on the tripod. All the others had gone aboard. And a score of blue globe-ships, like little sapphire moons, were circling a few thousand feet above, drifting around and a round, with a slow gliding motion, like buzzards circling over their carrion-prey.

The Prince had buried his face in his hands, standing in an attitude of utter dejection.

Bill turned, looked over the red flat sand of the Martian desert. Far below, leading toward the near horizon, he saw a winding line of footprints, half obliterated by the recent dust storm. Far away they vanished below the blue-black sky.

"Her tracks," he said, pointing.

"Tracks!" the Prince looked up, eager, hopeful determination flashing in his dark eyes. "Then we can follow... It may not be too late."

He ran toward the edge of the cliff.

Bill clutched his sleeve. "Wait! Think what you're doing, man! We're fighting to save the world. You can't run off that way. Anyhow, the sun is low. It is getting cool already. In two minutes after the sun goes down it will be cold as the devil. You'll die in the desert."

The Prince tugged away. "Hang the world. If you knew the way I feel about Paula—Lord, what a fool I've been. To drive her to this..."

Agony was written on his dark face; he bit his thin lip until blood oozed out and mingled indistinguishably with the red grime on his face. "Anyhow, the *vitomaton* is finished. Trainor can use it as well as I. I've got to find Paula—or die trying."

He started toward the brink of the precipice again. After the hesitation of a moment, Bill started after him. The Prince turned suddenly.

"What the devil are you doing here?"

"Well," said Bill, "the *Red Rover* is not a very attractive haven of refuge, with all those Martian ships flying around it. And I have come to think a good deal of Miss Paula. I'd like to help you find her."

"Don't come," said the Prince. "Probably it is death—"

"I'm not exactly an infant. I've been in tight places before. I've even an idea of what it would be like to die at night in this desert—I found the bones of a man in the dust today. But I want to go."

The Prince grasped Bill's hand. For a moment a tender smile of friendship came over the drawn mask of mingled despair and determination upon his lean face.

Presently the two of them found an inclining ledge that ran down the face of the red granite cliff, and scrambled along to the flat plain of acrid dust below. In desperate haste they plodded gasping along, following the scant traces of Paula's footprints that the storm had left. A hazy red cloud of dust rose about them, stinging their nostrils. They strangled and gasped for breath in the thin, dusty air. Sweaty grime covered them with a red crust.

For a mile they followed the trail. Then Paula had left the sand for a bare ledge of age-worn volcanic rock. The wind had erased what traces she might have left here. They skirted the edge of the ledge, but no prints were visible in the sand. The small red eye of the sun was just above the ocherous western rim of the planet. Their perspiring bodies shivered under the first chill of the frozen Martian night.

"It's no use," Bill muttered, sitting down on a block of timeworn granite, and wiping the red mud from his face. "She's probably been gone for hours. No chance."

"I've got to find her," the Prince cried, his lean, red-stained face tense with determination. "I'll circle about a little, and see if I can't pick up the trail."

Bill sat on the rock. He looked back at the low dark rim of cliffs, a mile behind, grim and forbidding against the somber, indigo sky. The crimson, melancholy splendor of the Martian sunset was fading in the west.

The silver sunship was out of sight behind the cliffs. But he could see the little blue globes, like spinning moons of sapphire, circling watchfully above it. They were lower now, some of them not a thousand feet above the hidden sunship.

Abruptly, one of them was enveloped in a vivid flare of orange light. Its blue gleam flickering out, and it fell in fragments of twisted white metal. Bill knew that it had been struck with a rocket torpedo.

The reply was quick and terrible. Slender, dazzling shafts of incandescent whiteness stabbed down toward the ship, each of them driving before it a tiny bright spark of purple fire, coruscating, iridescent.

They were the atomic bombs, Bill knew. A dozen of them must have been fired, from as many ships. In a few seconds he heard the reports of their explosions—in the thin, still air, they were mere sharp cracks, like pistol reports. They exploded below the line of his vision. No more torpedoes were fired from the unseen sunship. Bill could see nothing of it; but he was sure that it had been destroyed.

He heard the Prince's shout, thin and high in the rare atmosphere. It came from a hundred yards beyond him.

"I've found the trail."

Bill got up, trudged across to follow him. The Prince waited, impatiently, but gasping for breath. Just half of the red disk of the sun was visible in the indigo sky above the straight horizon, and a chill breeze blew upon them.

"I guess that ends the chance for the world," Bill gasped.

"I suppose so. Some fool must have shot that torpedo off, contrary to orders. The *vitomaton* might have saved us, if Trainor had had a chance to use it."

They plodded on through the dust, straining their eyes to follow the half-obliterated trail in the fading light. It grew colder very swiftly, for Mars has no such thick blanket atmosphere to hold the heat of day as has the earth.

Twilight was short. Splendid wings of somber crimson flame hung for a moment in the west. A brief golden glow shone where it had been. Then the sky was dark, and the million stars were standing out in cold, motionless majesty— scintillantly bright, unfeeling watchers of the drama in the desert.

Bill felt tingling cold envelope his limbs. The sweat and mud upon him seemed freezing. He saw the white glitter of frost appear suddenly upon his garments, even upon the red dust. The thin air he breathed seemed to freeze his lungs. He trembled. His skin became a stiff, numb, painful garment, hindering his movements. The Prince staggered on ahead of him, a vague dark shadow in the night, crying out at intervals in a queer, strained voice.

Bill stopped, looked back, shivering and miserable.

"No use to go on," he muttered. "No use." He stood still, vainly flapping his numb arms against his sides. A vivid picture came to him—a naked, staring, sun-bleached skull, lying in the red dust. "Bones in the dust," he muttered. "Bones in the dust. Envers' bones. And Paula's. The Prince's. Mine."

He saw something that made him stare, oblivious of the cold.

The red cliff had become a low dark line, below the star-studded sky. The score of little cobalt moons were still drifting around and around, in endless circles, watching, waiting. They were bright among the stars.

A little green cloud came up into view, above the dark rim of the cliff. A little spinning wisp of greenish vapor. A tiny sphere of swirling radiance. It shone with the clear lucent green of spring, of all verdure, of life itself. It spun, and it shone with live green light.

With inconceivable speed, it darted upward. It struck one of the blue globes. A sparkling mist of dancing emerald atoms flowed over the azure sphere, dissolved it, melted it away.

Bill rubbed his eyes. Where the sapphire ship had been was now only a swirling mass of green mist, a cloud of twinkling emerald particles, shining with a supernal viridescent radiance that somehow suggested *life*.

Abruptly as the first tiny wisp of green luminescence had appeared, this whirling cloud exploded. It burst into scores of tiny globes of sparkling, vibrant atoms. The green cloud had eaten and grown. Now it was reproducing itself like a living thing that feeds and grows and sends off spores.

And each of the little blobs of viridity flew to an azure sphere. It seemed to Bill as if the blue ships drew them—or as if the green globules of swirling mist were alive, seeking *food*.

In an instant, each swirling spiral of emerald mist had struck a blue globe. Vibrant green haze spread over every sphere. And the spheres melted, faded, vanished in clouds of swirling viridescent vapor.

It all happened very suddenly. It was hardly a second, Bill thought, after the first of the swirling green blobs had appeared, before the last of the Martian fliers had become a mass of incandescent mist. Then, suddenly as they had come, the green spirals vanished. They were blotted out.

The stars shone cold and brilliant, in many-colored splendor, above the dark line of the cliffs. The Martian ships were gone.

"The *vitomaton!*" Bill muttered. "The Prince said something about the *vitomaton*. A new weapon, using the force of life. And the green was like a living thing, consuming the spheres."

Suddenly he felt the bitter cold again. He moved, and his garments were stiff with frost. The cold had numbed his limbs—most of the pain had gone. He felt a curious lightness, an odd sense of relief, of freedom—and a delicious, alarming desire for sleep. But leaden pain of cold still lurked underneath, dull throbbing.

"Move. Move." he muttered through cold-stiffened lip. "Move. Keep warm."

He stumbled across the dust in the direction the Prince had taken. The cold tugged at him. His breath froze in swirls of ice. With all his will he fought the deadly desire for sleep.

He had not gone far when he came upon a dark shape in the night. It was the Prince, carrying Paula in his arms.

"I found her lying on the sand," he gasped to Bill. "She was awake. She was glad—forgave me—happy now."

The Prince was exhausted, struggling through the sand, burdened with the girl in his arms.

"Why go on?" Bill forced the words through his freezing face. "Never make it. They shot atomic bombs at *Red Rover*. Then something happened to them. Green light."

"The *vitomaton*," gasped the Prince. "Vortex of spinning, disintegrated atoms. Controlled by wireless power. Alive. Consumes all matter. Disintegrates it into atomic nothingness."

He staggered on toward the dark line of cliffs, clasping the inert form of the girl to his body.

"But Paula. I love her. I must carry her to the ship. It is my fault. We must get to the ship."

Bill struggled along beside him. "Too far," he muttered. "Miles, in the night. In the cold. We'll never—"

He stopped, with a thin, rasping cry.

Before him, above the narrow black line of the cliffs, a slender bar of luminescent silver had shot up into view. It was the slim, tapering cylinder of the *Red Rover,* with her twelve rear motor rays driving white and dazzling against the mountain she was leaving. The sunship, unharmed, driving upward into space!

"My God!" Bill screamed. "Leaving us!" He staggered forward, a pitiful, trembling figure, encased in stiff, frost-covered garments. He waved his arms, shouted. It was vain, almost ludicrous.

The Prince had stopped, still holding Paula in his arms.

"They think—Martians got us!" he called in a queer voice. "Stop them! Fire torpedo—at boulder. They will see!"

Bill heard the gasping voice. He unfastened the heavy tube that he still carried on his shoulder, leveled it before him. With numb, trembling fingers, he tried to move the levers. His fingers seemed frozen; they would not move. Tears burst from his eyes, freezing on his cheeks. He stood holding the heavy tube in his arms, sobbing like a baby.

Above them, the slender white cylinder of the *Red Rover* was driving out into star-gemmed space, dazzling opalescent rays shooting back at the dark mountain behind her.

"They go," Bill babbled. They think we are dead. Have not time to wait. Go to fight for world."

He collapsed in a trembling heap upon the loose, frosty sand.

The Prince had suddenly laid Paula on the ground, was beside him. "Lift the rocket," he gasped. "Aim. I will fire."

Bill raised the heavy tube mechanically, sighted through the telescope. His trembling was so violent that he could hardly hold it upon the rock. The Prince tried with his fingers to move the lever, in vain. Then he bent, pressed his chin against it. It slipped, cut a red gash in his skin. Again he tried, and the whir of the motor responded. He got his chin upon the little red button, pressed it. The empty shell drove back, fell from Bill's numbed hands and clattered on the sand.

The torpedo struck with a burst of orange light.

The Prince picked up Paula again, clasped her chilled body to him. Bill watched the *Red Rover*. Suddenly he voiced a glad, incoherent cry. The white rays that drove her upward were snapped out. The slim silver ship swung about, came down on a long swift glide.

In a moment, it seemed, she swept over them, with a searchlight sweeping the red sand. The white beam found the three. Quickly the ship dropped beside them. Grotesque figures in vacuum suits leapt from the air lock.

In a few seconds they were aboard, in warmth and light. Hot, moist air hissed into the lock about them, and they could breathe easily again. The sizzling of the air through the valves was the last impression of which Bill was conscious, until he found himself waking up in a comfortable bed, feeling warm and very hungry. Captain Brand was standing with his blue eyes peering through the door.

"Just looked in to see you as I was going on duty, Bill," he said. "Doctor Trainor says you're all right now. The Prince and Paula are too. You were all rather chilled, but nothing was seriously frozen. Lucky you shot off the rocket. We had given up hope for you didn't dare stay.

"Funny change has come over the Prince. He's been up a good while, sitting by Paula's bed. How's that for the misogynist—the hermit outlaw of space? Well, come on up to the bridge when you've had some breakfast. The battle with Mars is going to be fought out in the next few hours. Ought to be something interesting to see."

Having delivered his broadside of information so fast that the sleepy Bill could hardly absorb it, the bluff old space-captain withdrew his head, and went on.

An hour later Bill entered the bridge-room.

Gazing through the vitrolite panels, he saw the familiar aspect of interplanetary space—hard, brilliant points of many-colored light scintillating in a silver-dusted void of utter blackness. The flaming, red-winged sun was small and far distant. Earth was a huge green star, glowing with indescribably beautiful liquid emerald brilliance; the moon a silver speck beside it.

The grim red disk of Mars filled a great space in the heavens. Bill looked for a little blue dot that had been visible upon the red planet for so long—the tiny azure circle that he had first seen from the telescope in Trainor's Tower. He found the spot where it should be, on the upper limb of the planet. But it was gone.

"The thing has left Mars," Captain Brand told him. "It has set out on its mission of doom to Earth."

"What is it?"

"It is armored with one of their blue vibratory screens. What hellish contrivances of war it has in it, and what demoniac millions of Martians, no one knows. It is enormous, more than a mile in diameter."

"Can we do anything?"

"I hardly see how we can do anything. But we can try. Trainor and the Prince are coming with their *vitomaton.*"

"Say, didn't they shoot their atomic bombs at the ship last night?" Bill asked . "It was out of sight, but I imagined they had wrecked it."

"One of the lookouts who was late getting back brought down one of their globes with a rocket. They fired a lot of the purple bombs to scare us. But I think they meant to take us alive. In the interest of their science, I suppose. And Dr. Trainor got the *vitomaton* ready before they had done anything."

Bill was peering out into the star-strewn ebon gulf. Captain Brand pointed. He saw a tiny blue globe, swimming among the stars.

"There's the infernal thing. Carrying its cargo of horror to our earth."

In a few moments Dr. Trainor, the Prince, and Paula came one by one up the ladder to the bridge. Trainor carried the tripod; the Prince brought a little black case, which contained the strange vacuum tube with the cerium electrode, and its various accessories; Paula had a little calculating machine and a book of mathematical tables.

Trainor and the Prince set up the tripod in the center of the room, and mounted the little black case upon it. The apparatus looked not very different from a small camera. Working with cool, brisk efficiency, Paula began operating the calculating machine, taking numbers from the book, and calling out the results to the Prince, who was setting numerous small dials on the apparatus.

Dr. Trainor peered through a compact little telescope, which was evidently an auxiliary part of the apparatus, training the machine on the tiny blue disk that was the messenger of doom from Mars. From time to time he called out numbers, which seemed to go into Paula's calculations.

Looking curiously at Paula and the Prince, Bill could see no sign of an understanding between them. Both seemed absorbed in the problem before them. They were impersonal as any two collaborating scientists.

At last Dr. Trainor raised his eyes from the little telescope, and the Prince paused, with his fingers on a tiny switch. The induction coil, in the circuit of a powerful vitalium generator, was buzzing monotonously, while purple fire leapt between its terminals. Paula was still efficiently busy over the little calculating machine, pressing its keys while the motors whirred inside it.

"We're all ready," Trainor announced, "as soon as Paula finishes the integration." He turned to Bill and Captain Brand, who were eyeing the apparatus with intense interest. "If you will look inside this electron tube, when the Prince closes the switch, you will see a tiny green spark come into being. Just at the focus of the rays from the cerium electrode, inside the vitalium helix grid.

"That green spark is a living thing."

"It has in it the vital essence. It can consume matter—feed itself. It can grow. It can divide, reproduce itself. It responds to stimuli—it obeys the signals we send from this directional beam transmitter." He tapped an insignificant little drum.

"And it ceases to be, when we cut off the power.

"It is a living thing, that eats. And it is more destructive than anything else that eats, for it destroys the atoms that it takes into itself. It resolves them into pure vibratory energy, into free protons and electrons."

Paula called out another number, in her soft, husky voice. The Prince swiftly set a last dial, pressed a tiny lever. Bill, peering through the thin walls of a little electron tube, saw a filament light, saw the thin cerium disk grow incandescent, apparently under cathode bombardment. Then he saw a tiny green spark come into being, in a fine helix of gleaming vitalium wire. For a little time it hung there, swinging back and forth a little, growing slowly.

Deliberately, one by one, the Prince depressed keys on a black panel behind the tube. The little green spark wavered. Suddenly it shot forward, out through the wall of the tube. It swam uncertainly through the air in the room, growing until it was large as a marble. The Prince flicked down another key, and it darted out through a vitrolite panel, towards the blue globe from Mars.

It had cut a little round hole in the transparent crystal, a hole the size of a man's finger. The matter in it had vanished utterly. And the little viridescent cloud of curdled light that hung outside had grown again. It was as large as a man's fist—a tiny, whirling spiral of vibrant emerald particles.

Air hissed through the little hole, forming a frozen, misty cloud outside. Captain Brand promptly produced a little disk of soft rubber, placed it against the opening. Air-pressure held it tight, sealing the orifice.

The Prince pressed another key, the little swirling green sphere was whisked away—it vanished. The Prince stood intent, fingers on the banks of keys, eyes on red pointers that spun dizzily en tiny dials. Another key clicked down suddenly. He moved a dial, and looked expectantly out through the vitrolite panel.

Bill saw the green film run suddenly over the tiny blue globe floating among the stars. The azure sphere seemed to melt away, to dissolve into sparkling green radiance. In a moment, where the great blue ship had been, was only a spinning spiral of glistening viridescence.

"Look at Mars!" cried the Prince. "This is a challenge. If they want peace, they shall have it. If they want war, they shall feel the power of the *vitomaton!*"

Bill turned dazedly to look at the broad disk of the red planet. It was not relatively very far away. He could see the glistening white spot that was the north polar cap, the vast ocherous deserts, the dark equatorial markings, the green-black lines of the canals. For all the grimness of its somber, crimson color, it was very brilliant against the darkness of the spangled void.

An amazing change came swiftly over Mars.

A bluish tinge flowed over orange-red deserts. A thin blue mist seemed to have come suddenly into the atmosphere of the planet. It darkened, became abruptly solid. A wall of blue hid the red world. Mars became a colossal globe. Her surface was as real, as smooth and unbroken, as that of the ship they had just destroyed.

Mars had become a sphere of polished sapphire.

"A wall of vibration, I suppose," said the Prince. "What a science to condemn to destruction..."

Huge globes of purple fire—violet spheres large as the ship they had just destroyed—driven on mighty rays, leapt out from a score of points on the smooth azure armor that covered a world. With incredible speed, they converged toward the *Red Rover.*

"Atomic bombs with a vengeance!" cried the Prince. "One of those would throw the earth out of its orbit, into the sun." He turned briskly to Paula. "Quick now! Integrations for the planet!"

She sprang to the calculating machine; slim fingers flew over the keys. Trainor swung his apparatus toward the smooth azure ball that Mars had become, peered through his telescope, called out a series of numbers to Paula. Quickly she finished, gave her results to the Prince.

He bent over the banks of keys again.

Bill watched the enormous blue globe of Mars in fascinated horror, followed the huge, luminescent red-purple atomic bombs, that were hurtling out toward them, driven on broad white rays.

"An amazing amount of power in those atomic bombs," Dr. Trainor commented, his mild eyes bright with scientific enthusiasm. "I doubt that space itself is strong enough to hold up under their explosion. If they hit us, I imagine it will break down the continuum, blow us out of the universe altogether, out of space and time…"

Bill was looking at the whirling green spiral that hung where the Martian flier had been. He saw it move suddenly, dart across the star-dusted darkness of space. It plunged straight for the blue ball of Mars, struck it. A viridescent fog ran quickly over the enormous azure globe.

Mars melted away.

The planet dissolved in a huge, madly spinning cloud of brilliant green mist that shone with an odd light—with a light of *life!* A world faded into a nebulous spiral of green. Mars became a spinning cloud of dust as if of malachite.

A tiny lever flicked over, under the Prince's fingers. And the green light went out.

Where Mars had been was nothing! The stars shone through, hot and clear. A machine no larger than a camera had destroyed a world. Bill was dazed, staggered.

Solemnly, almost sadly, the Prince moved a slender, tanned hand over his brow. "A terrible thing," he said slowly. "It is a terrible thing to destroy a world. A world eons in the making, and that might have changed the history of the cosmos... But they voted for war. We had no choice."

He shook his head suddenly, and smiled. "It's all over. The great mission of my life—completed. Doctor I want you to pack the *vitomaton* very carefully, and lock it up in our best safe, and try to forget the combination. A great invention. But I hope we never need to use it again."

Then the Prince of Space did a thing that was amazing to most of his associates as the destruction of Mars had been. He walked quickly to Paula Trainor, and put his arms around her. He slowly tilted up her elfin face, where the golden eyes were laughing now, with a great, tender light of gladness shining in them. He bent, and kissed her warm red lips, with a hungry eagerness that was almost boyish.

A happy smile was dancing in his eyes when he looked up at the astounded Captain Brand and the others.

"Allow me," he said, "to present the Princess of Space!"

Some months later, when Bill was landed on Trainor's Tower, on a visit from his new home in the City of Space, he found the destruction of Mars had created a huge sensation. Astronomers were manfully inventing fantastic hypotheses to explain why the red planet had first turned blue, then green, and finally vanished utterly. The sunships of the Moon Patrol were still hunting merrily for the Prince of Space. Since the loss of the *Triton's* treasure, the reward for his capture had been increased to twenty-five million eagles.

THE END

If you've enjoyed this book, you will not want to miss these terrific titles…

ARMCHAIR SCI-FI, FANTASY, & HORROR DOUBLE NOVELS, $12.95 each

D-1   **THE GALAXY RAIDERS** by William P. McGivern
             SPACE STATION #1 by Frank Belknap Long

D-2   **THE PROGRAMMED PEOPLE** by Jack Sharkey
             SLAVES OF THE CRYSTAL BRAIN by William Carter Sawtelle

D-3   **YOU'RE ALL ALONE** by Fritz Leiber
             THE LIQUID MAN by Bernard C. Gilford

D-4   **CITADEL OF THE STAR LORDS** by Edmund Hamilton
             VOYAGE TO ETERNITY by Milton Lesser

D-5   **IRON MEN OF VENUS** by Don Wilcox
             THE MAN WITH ABSOLUTE MOTION by Noel Loomis

D-6   **WHO SOWS THE WIND…** by Rog Phillips
             THE PUZZLE PLANET by Robert A. W. Lowndes

D-7   **PLANET OF DREAD** by Murray Leinster
             TWICE UPON A TIME by Charles L. Fontenay

D-8   **THE TERROR OUT OF SPACE** by Dwight V. Swain
             QUEST OF THE GOLDEN APE by Ivar Jorgensen and Adam Chase

D-9   **SECRET OF MARRACOTT DEEP** by Henry Slesar
             PAWN OF THE BLACK FLEET by Mark Clifton.

D-10   **BEYOND THE RINGS OF SATURN** by Robert Moore Williams
             A MAN OBSESSED by Alan E. Nourse

ARMCHAIR SCIENCE FICTION CLASSICS, $12.95 each

C-1   **THE GREEN MAN**
             by Harold M. Sherman

C-2   **A TRACE OF MEMORY**
             By Keith Laumer

C-3   **INTO PLUTONIAN DEPTHS**
             by Stanton A. Coblentz

ARMCHAIR MASTERS OF SCIENCE FICTION SERIES, $16.95 each

M-1   **MASTERS OF SCIENCE FICTION, Vol. One**
             Bryce Walton—"Dark of the Moon" and other tales

M-2   **MASTERS OF SCIENCE FICTION, Vol. Two**
             Jerome Bixby—"One Way Street" and other tales

If you've enjoyed this book, you will not want to miss these terrific titles…

ARMCHAIR SCI-FI & HORROR DOUBLE NOVELS, $12.95 each

ARMCHAIR SCIENCE FICTION CLASSICS, $12.95 each

ARMCHAIR SCIENCE FICTION & HORROR GEMS SERIES, $12.95 each

If you've enjoyed this book, you will not want to miss these terrific titles...

ARMCHAIR SCI-FI, FANTASY, & HORROR DOUBLE NOVELS, $12.95 each

D-21   **EMPIRE OF EVIL** by Robert Arnette
       THE SIGN OF THE TIGER by Alan E. Nourse & J. A. Meyer

D-22   **OPERATION SQUARE PEG** by Frank Belknap Long
       ENCHANTRESS OF VENUS by Leigh Brackett

D-23   **THE LIFE WATCH** by Lester del Rey
       CREATURES OF THE ABYSS by Murray Leinster

D-24   **LEGION OF LAZARUS** by Edmond Hamilton
       STAR HUNTER by Andre Norton

D-25   **EMPIRE OF WOMEN** by John Fletcher
       ONE OF OUR CITIES IS MISSING by Irving Cox

D-26   **THE WRONG SIDE OF PARADISE** by Raymond F. Jones
       THE INVOLUNTARY IMMORTALS by Rog Phillips

D-27   **EARTH QUARTER** by Damon Knight
       ENVOY TO NEW WORLDS by Keith Laumer

D-28   **SLAVES TO THE METAL HORDE** by Milton Lesser
       HUNTERS OUT OF TIME by Joseph E. Kelleam

D-29   **RX JUPITER SAVE US** by Ward Moore
       BEWARE THE USURPERS by Geoff St. Reynard

D-30   **SECRET OF THE SERPENT** by Don Wilcox
       CRUSADE ACROSS THE VOID by Dwight V. Swain

ARMCHAIR SCIENCE FICTION CLASSICS, $12.95 each

C-7   **THE SHAVER MYSTERY, Book One**
      by Richard S. Shaver

C-8   **THE SHAVER MYSTERY, Book Two**
      by Richard S. Shaver

C-9   **MURDER IN SPACE**
      by David V. Reed

ARMCHAIR MASTERS OF SCIENCE FICTION SERIES, $16.95 each

M-3   **MASTERS OF SCIENCE FICTION, Vol. Three**
      Robert Sheckley, "The Perfect Woman" and other tales

M-4   **MASTERS OF SCIENCE FICTION, Vol. Four**
      Mack Reynolds, Part One, "Stowaway" and other tales

If you've enjoyed this book, you will not want to miss these terrific titles…

If you've enjoyed this book, you will not want to miss these terrific titles…

ARMCHAIR SCI-FI, FANTASY, & HORROR DOUBLE NOVELS, $12.95 each

D-41   **FULL CYCLE** by Clifford D. Simak
            IT WAS THE DAY OF THE ROBOT by Frank Belknap Long

D-42   **THIS CROWDED EARTH** by Robert Bloch
            REIGN OF THE TELEPUPPETS by Daniel Galouye

D-43   **THE CRISPIN AFFAIR** by Jack Sharkey
            THE RED HELL OF JUPITER by Paul Ernst

D-44   **PLANET OF DREAD** by Dwight V. Swain
            WE THE MACHINE by Gerald Vance

D-45   **THE STAR HUNTER** by Edmond Hamilton
            THE ALIEN by Raymond F. Jones

D-46   **WORLD OF IF** by Rog Phillips
            SLAVE RAIDERS FROM MERCURY by Don Wilcox

D-47   **THE ULTIMATE PERIL** by Robert Abernathy
            PLANET OF SHAME by Bruce Elliot

D-48   **THE FLYING EYES** by J. Hunter Holly
            SOME FABULOUS YONDER by Phillip Jose Farmer

D-49   **THE COSMIC BUNGLERS** by Geoff St. Reynard
            THE BUTTONED SKY by Geoff St. Reynard

D-50   **TYRANTS OF TIME** by Milton Lesser
            PARIAH PLANET by Murray Leinster

ARMCHAIR SCIENCE FICTION CLASSICS, $12.95 each

C-13   **SUNKEN WORLD**
            by Stanton A. Coblentz

C-14   **THE LAST VIAL**
            by Sam McClatchie, M. D.

C-15   **WE WHO SURVIVED (THE FIFTH ICE AGE)**
            by Sterling Noel

ARMCHAIR MASTERS OF SCIENCE FICTION SERIES, $16.95 each

MS-5   **MASTERS OF SCIENCE FICTION, Vol. Five**
            Winston K. Marks—Test Colony and other tales

MS-6   **MASTERS OF SCIENCE FICTION, Vol. Six**
            Fritz Leiber—Deadly Moon and other tales

If you've enjoyed this book, you will not want to miss these terrific titles…

ARMCHAIR SCI-FI & HORROR DOUBLE NOVELS, $12.95 each

ARMCHAIR SCIENCE FICTION & FANTASY CLASSICS, $12.95 each

If you've enjoyed this book, you will not want to miss these terrific titles…

ARMCHAIR SCI-FI & HORROR DOUBLE NOVELS, $12.95 each

D-71 **THE DEEP END** by Gregory Luce
TO WATCH BY NIGHT by Robert Moore Williams

D-72 **SWORDSMAN OF LOST TERRA** by Poul Anderson
PLANET OF GHOSTS by David V. Reed

D-73 **MOON OF BATTLE** by J. J. Allerton
THE MUTANT WEAPON by Murray Leinster

D-74 **OLD SPACEMEN NEVER DIE!** John Jakes
RETURN TO EARTH by Bryan Berry

D-75 **THE THING FROM UNDERNEATH** by Milton Lesser
OPERATION INTERSTELLAR by George O. Smith

D-76 **THE BURNING WORLD** by Algis Budrys
FOREVER IS TOO LONG by Chester S. Geier

D-77 **THE COSMIC JUNKMAN** by Rog Phillips
THE ULTIMATE WEAPON by John W. Campbell

D-78 **THE TIES OF EARTH** by James H. Schmitz
CUE FOR QUIET by Thomas L. Sherred

D-79 **SECRET OF THE MARTIANS** by Paul W. Fairman
THE VARIABLE MAN by Philip K. Dick

D-80 **THE GREEN GIRL** by Jack Williamson
THE ROBOT PERIL by Don Wilcox

ARMCHAIR SCIENCE FICTION CLASSICS, $12.95 each

C-25 **THE STAR KINGS**
by Edmond Hamilton

C-26 **NOT IN SOLITUDE**
by Kenneth Gantz

C-32 **PROMETHEUS II**
by S. J. Byrne

ARMCHAIR SCIENCE FICTION & HORROR GEMS SERIES, $12.95 each

G-7 **SCIENCE FICTION GEMS, Vol. Four**
Jack Sharkey and others

G-8 **HORROR GEMS, Vol. Four**
Seabury Quinn and others

If you've enjoyed this book, you will not want to miss these terrific titles…

ARMCHAIR SCI-FI, FANTASY, & HORROR DOUBLE NOVELS, $12.95 each

D-81   **THE LAST PLEA** by Robert Bloch
         THE STATUS CIVILIZATION by Robert Sheckley

D-82   **WOMAN FROM ANOTHER PLANET** by Frank Belknap Long
         HOMECALLING by Judith Merril

D-83   **WHEN TWO WORLDS MEET** by Robert Moore Williams
         THE MAN WHO HAD NO BRAINS by Jeff Sutton

D-84   **THE SPECTRE OF SUICIDE SWAMP** by E. K. Jarvis
         IT'S MAGIC, YOU DOPE! by Jack Sharkey

D-85   **THE STARSHIP FROM SIRIUS** by Rog Phillips
         FINAL WEAPON by Everett Cole

D-86   **TREASURE ON THUNDER MOON** by Edmond Hamilton
         TRAIL OF THE ASTROGAR by Henry Haase

D-87   **THE VENUS ENIGMA** by Joe Gibson
         THE WOMAN IN SKIN 13 by Paul W. Fairman

D-88   **THE MAD ROBOT** by William P. McGivern
         THE RUNNING MAN by J. Holly Hunter

D-89   **VENGEANCE OF KYVOR** by Randall Garrett
         AT THE EARTH'S CORE by Edgar Rice Burroughs

D-90   **DWELLERS OF THE DEEP** by Don Wilcox
         NIGHT OF THE LONG KNIVES by Fritz Leiber

ARMCHAIR SCIENCE FICTION CLASSICS, $12.95 each

C-28   **THE MAN FROM TOMORROW**
         by Stanton A. Coblentz

C-29   **THE GREEN MAN OF GRAYPEC**
         by Festus Pragnell

C-30   **THE SHAVER MYSTERY, Book Four**
         by Richard S. Shaver

ARMCHAIR MASTERS OF SCIENCE FICTION SERIES, $16.95 each

MS-7   **MASTERS OF SCIENCE FICTION AND FANTASY, Vol. Seven**
         Lester del Rey, "The Band Played On" and other tales

MS-8   **MASTERS OF SCIENCE FICTION, Vol. Eight**
         Milton Lesser, "'A' as in Android" and other tales

AN EARTH-SHAKING CHANGE IN THE WORLD'S POWER

The days of hydroelectric dams were over. But there was absolutely no assurance during the endless days of the future that the use of cosmic power was going to remain perpetually in place. And with the change in the control of this power came, by natural order, changes in economic and even in social control—violently. For the destiny of the world depended largely upon that commodity known as "power" and the men—good or evil—who controlled it.

Harl Vincent, one of the great authors of the golden age of science fiction, and who was himself an authority on the subject of electricity and power and their attendant social significance, conjured up an astonishing story filled with amazing action, taut intrigue, and the possibility of profound changes in mankind's future.

CAST OF CHARACTERS

SCOTT TERRIS
He was just another physicist from the upper levels—until one day the ability to change the world fell into his lap.

GAIL DESTINN
There was a calmness about him, a calmness that masked his intense drive, yet spoke of his utter brilliance.

NORINE ROSOV
In her heart was a bitterness toward all men of the upper levels, and it locked her heart from the man she truly loved.

ARTHUR MASON
It took a prison cell in a gigantic outer space globe to change the ways of this spoiled bureaucrat from evil to good.

MATT CRAWFORD
His lust for power was so great that he was willing to sell out his own people—but it soon got him far more than he bargained for!

PRESIDENT OWENS
He was president of the most powerful nation in the world, yet in reality he was nothing more than a masthead.

WILSON
Good old Wilson…a trusted servant who stood by his master through thick and thin.

POWER

By
HARL VINCENT

ARMCHAIR FICTION
PO Box 4369, Medford, Oregon   97501-0168

*For more information about Armchair Books and products, visit our
website at…*

www.armchairfiction.com

Or email us at…

armchairfiction@yahoo.com

CHAPTER ONE
The Darkness Before

NIGHT, whose magic was unknown in the levels below, was a thing of wondrous beauty when viewed from the continuous rooftops of twenty-third century New York. To the wearers of the gray, in the lowest levels of all, it was only a word, a vaguely disturbing term for one of the strange moods of nature that brought darkness and terror to the mysterious wilderness and jungles of the uninhabitable territory that lay between the great cities of United North America.

They shivered in dread of the darkness, that multitude in gray denim, for daylight was always with them; the artificial daylight of the Power Syndicate that came to them as unfailingly as did the humidified and iodized air they breathed. Of the same intensity and blue-white color throughout each twenty-four hours, it searched out every nook and cranny of the maze of passages and shaftways that separated as well as connected their living and working quarters. It was with them even as they slept; for them there was neither night nor day, only the passing of time.

But the wearers of the purple were more fortunate; for those so wealthy or favored as to reside in the topmost levels there was the opportunity of faring forth on the vast roof surface, where they might feast their eyes on the beauties of the heavens by night, if they so desired. A view of the moon and the stars, or the grandeur of a storm-tossed sky shot with luminous streaks, that were the night-flying ships of the government lines, was theirs for the asking. But there were few who availed themselves of the privilege; the rigors of nature were not to be braved with impunity by those whose bodies were accustomed to the uniform temperature and humidity of the interior, whose eyes were unused to the darkness and ears to the murmuring silence of the outside world.

Scott Terris, that virile and brilliant young physicist, who was chief of the Science Research Bureau, had long made a habit of taking nightly walks along the railed footpath that skirted the edge of the fifteen hundred foot precipice that was the west wall of windowless, steel-cased New York. Here it was that his mind worked at its best; away from the muffled roar and the carefully regulated synthetic existence of the interior, his vast accumulation of scientific deductions of the day's research could be marshaled in orderly array to form the basis of some new theory or discovery that would startle the Americas on the following morning.

Tonight was an exception. The moonlit ripples of the Hudson River, and the sweet-scented breeze that drifted over from the forestlands, which extended to the very edge of the Palisades on the Jersey side, had none of their usual soothing effect. A solitary muffled figure, he dallied near the trapdoor that opened into his private laboratory below, his thoughts in an unwonted turmoil of vague unrest.

The pulsating life of the great city made itself felt in the metal plates beneath his feet. Fifty million souls there were, down there in that seething hive of industry and idle folly, of hopeless ignorance and scintillating genius, of monotonous routine existences and pleasure-mad lives. Sixty-five levels crammed with those of the gray denim, thirty levels of the soulless mechanicals, and five where the wearers of the purple dwelt in the utmost prodigality of freedom and spaciousness. And everywhere there were the red police. One city of the eight of equal size now housed the entire population of United North America. It was an artificial life;

concentration of the inhabitants to the *nth* degree, and utter waste of the land that lay between.

He was startled from his reverie by a sharp detonation somewhere below—in his laboratory, it seemed. But the place was deserted; it had been for hours. In the next instant he was at the trapdoor, his eyes straining in the effort to pierce the gloom of the huge workroom.

A sudden blinding light-shaft sprang into being as the door of one of his electric furnaces was opened. There was the momentary glimpse of a muscular arm and a hand that gripped a slender pair of tongs in callused fingers. There was the withdrawal of a tiny crucible from the white heat of the furnace, and the sliding back of the door, and then the crucible was a dazzling light fleck that danced through the blackness toward one of the workbenches.

Scott slipped down the iron ladder and fumbled for the light button, flooding the laboratory with its normal sunglow illumination. He could scarcely believe his eyes when they rested on the figure that bent over the sizzling crucible. A powerfully built young fellow, in the gray denim of fifty levels below, straightened up quickly at the coming of the light and faced him, surprised but unafraid.

"What are you doing here?" Terris snapped, his amazement overcome by a rising flood of indignation.

The intruder lay aside his tongs with calm deliberation, grinning suddenly in disarming fashion. "Oh," he said softly, "just working on a little idea of my own. I didn't expect you back for an hour."

"Didn't expect me back!" Scott exploded. "You have your nerve breaking into my place and—"

He was advancing toward the astonishing young fellow in gray, his emotions alternating between deep curiosity as to the meaning of the intrusion and grim determination to deal summarily with the sneaking workman—to turn him over to the red police. But there was something in the intruder's level gaze that gave him pause.

Remarkably keen gray eyes regarded him from underneath a tousled thatch of flaming red hair. And in those eyes there lurked a fixity of purpose that was overwhelming in its intensity, a hint of the indomitable will of the possessor and of almost fanatical devotion to some great impelling ambition that was the primal urge of his being. Stern eyes, and knowing, yet they smiled into his own. Scott's wrath evaporated.

"Sorry you caught me," his visitor said in even tones. "I had hoped to accomplish something before that happened. And I might tell you that I have done no harm here, nor have I taken anything from the laboratory at any time."

"At any time!" Scott exclaimed blankly. "Then you have been here before—often perhaps?"

"Oh yes." He was a strange anomaly, this wearer of the gray, and obviously had risen far above his station. He studied Scott's expression carefully for a moment; then, "I'm Gail Destinn," he said. "Perhaps I'd better explain."

"I think you had," Scott returned, forcing the assumption of what he considered a tone of severity. In spite of himself he was enjoying the encounter; this Destinn was a likable chap, and his self-assurance and poise were so serenely unaffected as to compel respect. It was incredible that one who wore the gray should have developed these qualities; that he should display the scientific knowledge and aptitude evidenced by his nocturnal activities.

"Yes," Destinn was saying thoughtfully, "I owe you an explanation and an apology as well." He hesitated, and his eyes strayed to a corner of the room where a hidden panel was open, revealing the cage of a gravity-control lift. "Mr. Terris," he blurted out, "you look to be a good scout. I wonder if you'd consent to taking a trip down below with me;

let me show you something of the life of my kind and of what is going on down there in the lower levels. I can explain much better then, and I'm sure you'll not think the time wasted."

Scott stared in amazement at the open panel in the wall of his supposedly secret retreat. A concealed shaftway connected his laboratory with the lower levels! He saw that his uninvited guest awaited his reply with poorly concealed eagerness. And there was sincerity of purpose and a longing for friendly understanding in his anxious gaze.

"All right, Destinn," he decided, "I'll go with you. And I know I'll enjoy the visit."

SCOTT TERRIS was a man who had given little thought to those who inhabited the lower levels; he had never been below the levels of the mechanicals and had had little contact with those of the gray denim, with the exception of a few menials in his own household and those who tended the mechanicals of the intermediate sections. He knew there was poverty and ignorance among them, of course, and knew of the troubles of the red police when they became unruly down there. But his science was an exacting taskmaster, crowding from his waking thoughts all alien considerations. True, he loved humanity—collectively—and strove for its betterment in all things that science could provide. But, as an individual, man had taken little place in his interest.

As the cage of the lift dropped swiftly into the depths of its shaft, he appraised the straight youthful figure of Gail Destinn with something of envy in his heart. Suddenly it came to him that there was much in life that he had missed— much that he was missing. Apparently the gray-clad workers felt less of the monotony of existence than did he; perhaps even his pleasure-mad fellows of the purple were wiser in their pursuits than he had suspected. Certainly, he was thrilling to the novelty of this situation and to the sense of adventure that came with the swift descent into regions unknown.

They stepped out into a narrow corridor when the lift came to rest and Scott followed mechanically when his host led the way to a tiny cubicle, which proved to be his sleeping quarters. Scott marveled that a human being could live and think sanely in the crowded space.

"Not much of a place, Mr. Terris," Gail Destinn apologized, "but it serves its purpose. Here, sir, you'd better put these on before we go out in the Square."

He grinned engagingly as he tossed a suit of the despised gray denim on the cot; then sat cross-legged on the floor as Scott nodded his understanding.

"You see," he explained, "I want you to observe things as they are, and everyone would shut up like government witnesses if they saw you out there in the purple. I'd like you to listen to some of the conversation in the ways and other public places before I tell you of the experiment I'm working on."

Scott Terris struggled with the buttonless gray shirt, emerging with a grunt of relief when he finally conquered the thing. "Experiment?" he asked. "You were using my laboratory in some research work of your own?" Strange that he could feel no animosity toward this smiling youth who had so calmly invaded his sanctum and then inveigled him into this visit.

"Why yes, of course. That furnace, you see, is the only one in existence that is capable of producing the extreme temperature I need. I simply had to have access to it, and I knew the only way of getting it was to take it. The forgotten shaftway made it easy."

"I see." Scott frowned in perplexity; he didn't see. That particular furnace was used only for involved research into the structure of the atom. This Destinn couldn't possibly...

"What the devil are you up to, Gail?" a gruff voice broke in from the doorway. "I thought you were at work up top."

"I was," Destinn replied suavely, his hand moving to Scott's arm with swift warning pressure. "Had to quit early to meet my friend."

"Oh yeah! And who's he?"

Scott turned to look at the stocky, blue-jowled man who regarded him with suspicion, if not with open antagonism. Gail, with a quick movement, had hidden the discarded purple raiment and now faced the newcomer with easy confidence.

"Firmin—Bill Firmin, from the forty-ninth level," he said evenly. "You've heard me speak of him, Tom. Shake hands, you two. Bill, I want you to know Tom Prouty, our ward leader here."

A flabby hand was stretched there before him, and as Scott hesitated, he saw Gail Destinn's jaw muscles tense spasmodically. There must be a hidden danger here; this Prouty had a sinister look about him that was not at all in keeping with the direct frankness of young Destinn. But the younger fellow was afraid of Prouty for some reason; Scott saw those taut jaw muscles relax in a relieved smile when he took the cold limp hand of the politician in his own.

"Glad to know you, Bill," said Prouty. "If you're a friend of Gail's, I suppose you're all right. And, take it from me, big boy, you'd better be right; things are popping pretty soon and you guys in the forties better be with us."

"Bill's the best there is, Tom," Destinn interposed hastily. "I'm taking him over to the Square with me."

"Well, make it snappy," Prouty growled. "May do him some good. Meeting's on, you know, and Sarovin is talking tonight. Afterwards I want to see you in my office alone—don't bring this guy along."

For a moment Scott thought his young host was about to explode. But Prouty scowled him down; then turned on his heel and was gone.

"I'm sorry, Mr. Terris," Destinn whispered. "I've let you in for something, I'm afraid. Tom's a bad actor, and he's suspicious of you. Guess we'd better get you back up top where you belong."

"You mean I'm to run away?" Scott's blood boiled at the idea of sneaking off in fear of this ignorant bully. "Not on your life!" he grated. "I'm here now, and here I stay until I learn what it's all about. Let's go to this Square of yours."

Young Destinn grinned anew and his fine eyes twinkled. "You are a good scout," he breathed delightedly. "Come on—Bill."

Responding somehow to the savage call of the danger he saw ahead, Scott Terris followed eagerly when his new friend dashed off down the corridor toward the moving way.

CHAPTER TWO
The Storm

THEY found a sizable gathering of the gray-clad workers in one corner of the Square whose massive columns extended from the fiftieth to the sixtieth levels in the Food Company section. A fiery little hunchback, with abnormally large head and long arms that waved in wild gestures as he talked, was addressing them from a platform near one of the public newscasting stations. His voice was raised in harsh competition with the announcer's, and the attention of his audience strayed ever and anon to the changing views on the bright screen.

"Sarovin," Gail Destinn whispered hoarsely, "the most dangerous agitator we have down here. Notice how the police watch him?"

Scott saw that a half dozen of the red-coated guards were close by, far more alert in their interest than was usual. These meetings of the workers, which were numerous, were smiled upon by the authorities and rarely occasioned them serious concern. But this Sarovin, one knew instinctively, was a personage, a power; there was an ominous note in his voice, a ring of insolent defiance, that carried with it the assurance that comes only with the certainty of powerful backing and political protection.

"Comrades," he was shouting, "I call upon you now to give up this milk-and-water plan of the Council of Five and their scientists. As things are going, it will be years before results are obtained—if ever they are. Forget it, I say; let us rise in our might and take what is ours. We have earned it by the sweat of our brows, this vast wealth that is in the hands of the few who wear the purple. We, who toil for a pittance that they may live their lives of luxury and ease; we, whom they consider as inferior to the mechanicals and as dust beneath their feet—we have made of this so-called republic a power so great that the entire world is prostrate before us. And they have taken it from us, these bloated plutocrats of the upper levels. It is high time we asserted ourselves, comrades, and there is only one way of regaining what is rightfully ours—by force. I am here to tell you that force is to be used; blood must be spilled in the cause. Blood, I tell you! It is only with their lives that they can pay for what they have done. And the time is at hand."

"Easy there, Sarovin," a lieutenant of the red police called out good-naturedly, "that's becoming a bit strong."

Gail Destinn gripped Scott's arm with fingers that trembled, and his face was flushed to match the hue of his tousled thatch. There were rumblings of approval from the audience, and eyes no longer were turned to the screen of the newscasts. Sarovin had struck answering chords in the breasts of his hearers.

"To hell with the police!" a voice thundered. "Go on, Sarovin!"

"There spoke a man," the hunchback gloated. "If the rest of you had half his guts there'd be nothing to it. Why listen, comrades, the red police can't stop us; neither can those of the purple. Think of our many millions, aroused, and of the handful with whom we have to deal. After all, there are only a score or so we must get out of the way—the President and his cabinet, who are but tools of the Power Syndicate—Matt Crawford, the real Dictator, and—"

"Sarovin! Wait—you're crazy!" Young Destinn was ploughing his way through the milling crowd toward the platform, despite hands that clutched and voices that screeched in protest.

The lieutenant of red police yelled an order to his men and they bored into the crowd with maces swinging. Instant uproar echoed in the Square as the shriek of a siren rang out in frantic call for police reserves. A swelling cadence of angry voices came booming from the balconies surrounding the enclosure at the levels above.

There was the popping of riot pistols in the hands of the red police, and the gurgling bursts of their rubbery missiles, as twining tentacles spurted forth to imprison the flailing arms of the workers and bring them helpless to the pavement. From the vaulted reaches overhead, cable cars of the police swooped down as the wearers of the gray streamed into the Square in ever-increasing number.

"Comrades!" Destinn was shouting from the platform, where he held Sarovin squirming in his long arms. "Don't listen to this fool. It'll mean war if you do; murder and destruction—rapine—"

"Let it be war!" Sarovin screamed, and Gail clamped a huge hand over his mouth.

"No!" he bellowed. "There's a better way. And it won't take years, either. We're almost ready now to lick the Power Syndicate at their own game. This cosmic energy of theirs will be supplanted by a source we will control. Their sting will be gone then, and we'll have the situation in hand—peaceably."

His words fell on unheeding ears or were drowned out by the cries of the angry mob. Scott forced his way closer to the platform and saw that others were climbing over its edge. Tom Prouty, red of face and spouting profanity, was first to reach young Destinn. Something flashed bright in his hand, crackling spitefully. A needle-gun! One of those dread weapons of the war of 2212.

And then Gail Destinn was swaying there, clawing at the slender dart that had pierced his shoulder. Prouty, clubbing his pistol, was hammering away at him as his hands worked frantically to free the thing that even now glowed to its destroying incandescence and brought wisps of smoke curling from the flesh it scorched. But the ward leader's blows rained on him unnoticed; with a mighty wrench he tore the dart free and dashed it to the platform, where it sang its shrill song of death in the furious and murderous discharge of atomic energy.

Screeching in mortal terror as a dazzling spray of hissing metal cascaded from the platform, Tom Prouty flung himself into the mass of humanity that fell back in sudden blind panic. Fighting madly among themselves and against the cordon of red police that hemmed them in; trampling those of their number who were borne down by the crush, they retreated before the roaring inferno the energy needle had created by expending its mighty forces in the steel floorplates instead of in the human flesh for which it was intended.

Scott found himself alone, close by the consuming blast of molten particles. Destinn was dragging himself painfully away from the searing flame, his features contorted in agony and his right side useless in the paralysis that had gripped him.

"Look!" he gasped, when Scott reached him. "Up there—Sarovin! It got him." Then Gail Destinn collapsed and lay still.

The platform was sagging in blobs of flowing metal. And, standing erect in the white heat of the atomic blast that spouted there, was the thing that had been Sarovin. Like a flaming, bloated statue it stood there with arms outstretched as if to ward off the fires of hell that encompassed it. Pinpoints of flashing brilliance exploded rapidly in the distorted mass, and then, in a puff of swirling gases, it was gone.

There swelled a mighty roar from the throats of the thousands of gray-clad observers in the balconies. Voices, terrified and unintelligible at first, then coming in unison like a practiced and prearranged chorus of long-suppressed hatred.

"Down with those of the purple! Down with the government! It is Sarovin they've killed. Sarovin! Death to the President and to Crawford. Death in the upper levels!"

Dazed by the vast tumult of sound and awed by the tremor that assailed the huge structure of the city under the measured stamping of thousands of feet, Scott Terris gazed out over the scene with eyes that saw only its wider significance. Here was a tremendous force unleashed, a savage fury that would spread to every city in the country through the mysterious communication channels of the gray-clad multitude. A reign of terror in the making; civil war that would threaten the very foundations of the nation—of civilization itself.

FROM out the press of the howling mob there dashed a slim figure, a girl-figure in gray, who sped to kneel at Gail Destinn's side. Her swift white fingers explored his wounds and then she looked up with startled wide eyes to regard the tall stranger who stood there as if rooted to the spot. Rendered speechless by the quick revelation of the girl's fresh beauty, Scott was able only to smile in sickly fashion at her suddenly contemptuous stare.

"Are you a friend of his?" she asked.

"Why—why yes," he stammered.

"Then why don't you do something? He's terribly hurt—dying. Here, help me with him—if you can come out of your trance."

Suddenly Scott wanted more than anything else in the world to see young Destinn recover and to know more of this lovely bit of femininity in the gray of the sub-levels. Gail was conscious, he saw quickly, but was unable to move a muscle. The pain-glazed eyes regarded him with something of the beseeching look of a helpless dumb creature about to be used in a laboratory experiment.

With a swift return of his normal alertness, he lifted the limp form in his arms and straightened with a jerk. "All right," he growled in the girl's ear, "where'll I take him?"

"This way—hurry." The girl's voice was a bare whisper above the din of the Square. She pointed into the shadows of the great pillars where it seemed to be deserted of human presence.

The battle raged furiously behind them as they made their way in the direction she had indicated. The roaring destruction of the energy needle had spent itself and only a gaping opening, its edges cooled already to dull red heat, showed where it had fused its way through the floorplates into the level below. Fresh detachments of the red police were arriving continuously and it seemed that they were getting the situation in hand—temporarily at least.

"Here, to the westbound way," the girl was saying. "A dispensary is close by."

They were on the swiftly moving platform then, and Scott shifted his burden so that the wobbling head rested on his shoulder. Gail Destinn moaned feebly and mumbled words came from his lips.

"No, no," he objected. "Not to the dispensary. Take me—up top. To your laboratory, Terris. There is work—must be done."

The girl heard and understood. "You are Scott Terris," she exclaimed angrily. "Down here, wearing the gray and misleading poor Gail. Getting him into this terrible trouble. Well, you can just put him down, Mr. Terris. I'll see him to the dispensary myself."

"Terris, don't do it," Destinn begged. "Tell her it's all right. I must go on."

"Put him down at once," the girl snapped.

"Did you hear his last words?" Scott bridled.

"No," coldly aloof, "I didn't. But I know what's for his good."

Scott had little knowledge of the ways of the fair sex. Perhaps he would not have dared lose his temper as he did now, had he been more experienced. But he had made up his mind about Destinn and no mere woman could change it.

"Look here, young lady," he rasped, "I'm taking charge of this man. He's going up top as he desires, and my own physician will attend him. Get that?"

The girl faced him, white and speechless with indignation, as the moving platform sped on its smooth way to the west side. He thought he heard the injured man chuckle, but decided it was a cough.

"Thanks," Destinn whispered weakly. "Stay on this Way until you reach the turn. Norine will show you the entrance...to secret lift...she's a good sport...underneath..." A gasp of pain cut short his words and he lapsed into unconsciousness.

Across the corridor the eastbound way was suddenly jammed with vociferous crowds of the gray-clad workers. They had heard of the affair in the Square and were on their way to join forces with their fellows. A few there were who shouted over the intervening space, but for the most part they paid no attention to the little group on the westbound platform.

The girl Norine huddled closely to his side as if she feared she would be recognized. She stroked Destinn's limp hand now, but kept her eyes averted from his face.

In the next instant her slight body was racked with dry sobs.

CHAPTER THREE
Judgment

DOCTOR MOWRY shook his head gravely. "Your friend will live, Scott," he said, "but as a hopeless paralytic. He'll never walk again, nor will he be able to raise a finger to the simplest task. Normal nerve currents, you see, were blocked by the energy—permanently."

"You're sure there's no chance, Doc?" Sick at heart, Scott was grasping at straws. He had waited many hours in fearful anticipation of this verdict, but now he was unwilling to abide by it.

"Not a chance," the doctor asserted. "The usual experience in 2212, you'll recall. Even when they escaped the extreme penalty of the vicious needle energy, slightly wounded combatants were doomed to this living death of inactivity and impotence."

"Good lord! No wonder we abolished war and jettisoned all stocks of the needle guns." Scott sat thinking bitterly for a long time after the doctor left. He'd like to lay hands on this Prouty—a cowardly blackguard who would use one of the forbidden weapons on a man like Gail Destinn! Probably stole the thing from a museum.

The voice of the newscast announcer droned from the sound mechanism of his private visiphone. Colby, another of the cabinet members, had been assassinated. President Owens closely guarded in fresh outbreaks from sub-levels of Washington. Matt Crawford fleeing in a rocket car to one of his cosmic energy globes out there in the stratosphere. Another coward!

Snorting his disgust with conditions in general, Scott arose from his easy chair and made his way to the room where Destinn lay.

The girl Norine started noticeably at his entrance and moved from the bedside. Her eyes were red with weeping, but she tossed her head and averted her gaze when Scott addressed her.

"Has Gail been told?" he asked her gently.

A nod of grim assent was the girl's only reply, but the sick man answered in a tense whisper through lips that were white and pinched. "Yes, Terris, they told me."

He was silent then, but his eyes shone bright with that same indomitable spirit they had held when Scott first encountered him as an intruder in the laboratory.

"It's a tough break for me," he continued, "but my work isn't finished yet. Terris, I'd like you to help me."

"I'll do anything I can," Scott assured him, shakily.

"Norine, will you please leave us alone?" came from the pinched lips as the bright eyes caressed the drooping girl.

She left silently and the sick man looked long and earnestly at the famous scientist of the upper levels. "You've done much for me, Terris," he said then, "More than I can tell you. And, somehow, I feel that you'll do more—for the real Cause."

"You mean that of the gray multitude?"

"I mean the cause of true Democracy; not what you saw exemplified last night. You know now that the workers are a class gone crazy under the oppression of the purple-clad minority—or rather I should say, of the capitalistic system. Yet they are fools, Terris, and so easily swayed as to make their foolishness dangerous. But I need not tell you of that; you saw for yourself. Already their mistaken and misled zeal is manifest in the carnage which has started and that may end in widespread disaster. It is to prevent such disaster that I am asking for your assistance."

"You speak of the alternative you mentioned when you shut off Sarovin down there?"

"Yes. And to explain further I will tell you what you must recognize of your own knowledge. Terris, our country is at the mercy of the Power Syndicate; Matt Crawford is the man who runs it to suit himself and his greedy associates. There is no true representation of the people in the government; even you who wear the purple must perforce do as Crawford dictates. And it pleases him to favor you who live up top; it adds to his own personal glory. But he and his 'yes-men' have nothing but contempt for those of the sub-levels; that and starvation wages, and the persecution of the red police is their lot. Am I right?"

"I hadn't thought much about it, Gail," Scott returned. "That is, not until last night. My interest, as you know, is wrapped up in science, but I'm beginning to see certain things in a new light. Go on with your story—if you can stand it."

"Oh, I'm all right; for talking, at least." The courageous lips actually twisted themselves into a smile. "The whole thing is wrong in principle, Terris. It goes back to the dark ages when first the concentration of wealth in the hands of the few became evident. We are not socialistic in these days; we know of the failure of the soviets in the twentieth century, and we know why they failed. Men were not created equal, and to those of superior aggression and mentality there must come superior reward. But not to the extent that now exists; and a disproportionate reward must not come to the undeserving through the efforts of others who are starved into submission. Do you follow me?"

"Sure." Scott was deeply interested; he never had approved of the grasping methods of the Power Syndicate.

"Forget the preliminaries," he said. "Let's come to this plan for a peaceable solution of the problem."

"Attaboy!" Destinn approved. "Since you put it that way, the idea is this: Crawford controls the power supply of United North America today. With the passing of the use of natural fuels, we were forced to turn to the cosmic rays of outer space for our power. Our very existence depends on this vast industry that Crawford acquired by inheritance and later financial manipulation. Were he to cut off the energy supply radiated to our cities from his globes that float out there in the stratosphere, we should perish. Our synthetic foods could not be produced, our artificial sunlight would die out; our heat, the essential labors of the mechanicals—all would stop. Everything we wear and use in this life to which we have become accustomed would automatically cease to exist for us as replaceable and renewable necessities. We should revert to a savage state and be compelled to venture out into the wilderness where most of us would perish. It is our vital need for power that gives Crawford the whip hand over us all."

"And to remedy this you propose—"

"Another and simpler source of power. Cheap and unlimited energy as the emancipator of our modern slaves. The death of this tyranny, and the return to a true republican form of government." The stricken idealist closed his lids and a blissful expression spread over his features.

Scott's interest as a scientist overcame any possible exception he might otherwise have taken. "This new energy," he suggested, "is to be obtained from the atom."

"Yes, but not by its disruption. All we have ever accomplished by destroying the atom is further destruction—of life or of other matter. Witness the sub-atomic energy of the needle gun."

Scott looked hastily away from the pain that came to replace the enthusiasm that had radiated from those fine eyes. But Destinn shook off the black mood instantly and continued:

"Terris, I can produce usable energy in inconceivable amounts by a building-up of atoms rather than by their disintegration. The method provides a virtual reproduction of cosmic ray energy. The birth of atoms radiates a tremendous force that we have learned how to use and control. Think of it... By building up only four grams of helium—about a seventh of an ounce—from hydrogen atoms, we release nuclear energy equivalent to a million horsepower for an hour. Duplicate the natural processes of outer space that give rise to this birth of atoms; force the hydrogen nuclei to combine with electrons to form helium nuclei and the vast energy release is effected. We manufacture our own cosmic rays, and our own energy, from practically nothing!"

"Yes, but try and do it." Scott was frankly skeptical.

"Terris, I can do it; I have done it! Listen..."

And Scott Terris listened while the sick man, in enthusiastic if somewhat weakening voice, expounded his theories and told of his hopes; explained the plans of the Council of Five, and detailed the results of the experiments already conducted.

AN hour later, convinced and marveling, Terris stepped forth into the corridor to come face to face with Norine Rosov.

In his excitement he failed to notice that the girl's finely chiseled features had regained their normal composure and that her color had returned. He did observe that the close-cropped golden hair gleamed with the luster imparted by a recent smoothing; that there was something less strained in her attitude. She was more at ease in his presence than she had been since their first meeting.

"He has talked with you of his plans?" she inquired.

"Indeed, he has, Miss Norine. And, since you are so deeply concerned in the important matter, I feel we should have an understanding without delay. Will you come into my library?"

There was no hesitation on the girl's part when she preceded him into the spacious and luxurious room, where it was his wont to retire in privacy for his studies. But there was a haunting something in her wide stare when she seated herself across from him, a hint of some fear of himself or of the surroundings, that she could not quite down. Her slim, white fingers trembled noticeably as she lighted a cigarette.

"Gail has asked that you be permitted to help me," he said in a strained voice he could not have accounted for.

"He tells me that you have helped him in the work and that you know a great deal about what he has done. Of course, you know that he wants me to go ahead with the experiments?"

"Yes; he told me. And you consented?"

"I did. I likewise agreed to use your knowledge and assistance in the work, providing, of course, this is satisfactory to you."

The girl frowned. "You are doing this," she asked, "for what purpose? Surely you have not espoused the cause of the gray-clad workers?"

"I'm doing it in the interest of science," he returned stiffly, "and of the general good to humanity that is involved. You need have no fear that it will work to the disadvantage of your comrades."

"You'll not betray us—betray Gail, I mean—to the Power Syndicate?" The girl's expression was dubious.

"Certainly not!" Scott flushed uncomfortably. It was impossible that he come out flatly in support of the gray multitude; too many of them were of the type of Tom Prouty or the one who had been known as Sarovin. Nor could he fully approve of the opposite side—his own fellows of the upper levels. There was justice and injustice, both up top and down below, with the wearers of the gray getting somewhat the worse of existing conditions. But how to explain this attitude of mind to this beauteous and imperious girl who regarded him with such open suspicion if not with actual dislike. How to...

"Gail trusts you," she broke in then, with a quick half-smile. "And, that being the case, I suppose I can. We start work at once?"

Surprised, Scott jumped to his feet with alacrity. It would be great to have the girl around, at that. "Right away!" he exclaimed. "And you'll make your home here?" Then, aghast at his own temerity, "To be near Gail, of course," he finished lamely.

"Yes—to be near Gail." The girl rose unsteadily and swift tears came trembling on her long lashes. An hysterical sob caught in her throat. "Poor, poor Gail," she moaned.

And Scott, moving with soft steps in deference to her feeling, made his way toward the laboratory.

CHAPTER FOUR
Accomplishment

VAGUELY disturbed by a realization of his growing concern over this girl who had come into his life under such trying circumstances, Scott set himself half-heartedly to the task of arranging his apparatus for the work that he must do. She was the compassionate mate of Gail Destinn, the paralyzed man had admitted, but it seemed apparent that the relationship was a one-sided arrangement. Certainly Destinn had not exhibited the depth of emotion one would have expected in the fortunate possessor of so beautiful and talented a companion.

Norine, on the other hand, was deeply and madly in love. That was quite evident from her bearing. She'd fight for her man like a tigress, if occasion demanded, and stick to him through thick and thin. To her it would not matter that he was no longer able to protect her; that his marvelous vitality of body had been taken from him in that horrible instant when the needle-energy struck him down. To a girl like that, the union was a permanent and sacred thing; a responsibility not to be cast aside. And yet she was, above all, a woman...primitive in her emotions and a creature of strange caprice. Intoxicating the senses in her exotic allure...chilling them to sub-zero frigidity in the next instant with her aloof disapproval...

Scott shook his head angrily and turned his eyes to the fluorescent screen of the radio-microscope. He'd have to keep his mind free of such thoughts. There was work to be done, important work, and he needed his every faculty under control.

The laboratory visiphone buzzed an insistent call and he flipped the lever that illuminated its disc. An anxious face appeared there, the face of his first assistant at the Research Bureau.

"When will you be at the Bureau offices?" the white lips asked.

"Not today, Warren," Scott returned impatiently. "I've something to do here. I may shut myself in for a week."

"But—but say! President Owens has called a conference. The devil's to pay, Terris. You'll have to come down."

"I can't. Tell 'em I'm sick; dead, if you want to—anything."

His eyes had strayed to the green-lit screen of the super-microscope, where a dazzling light-burst showed for an instant in the path of the theta rays, and then was gone. A single atom of helium created! The process was successful in its initial stage.

"But, Terris," the visiphone was pleading, "Crawford has returned. He's fighting mad, and he wants you to—"

"Oh, damn Crawford! Tell him I refuse!" The visiphone disc went dark and the panicky voice broke off as he slammed the lever back.

So Matt Crawford was taking up the challenge of the gray-clad multitude—and wanting him to do some of his dirty work of reprisal, Scott thought grimly. This was to be war all right; the civil war Destinn had predicted, with bloodshed and misery—the Lord only knew what might happen with Crawford's diabolical mind at work. And Scott was in the middle, he knew; he'd be cast off by his fellows of the purple for his defection, and scorned by those of the gray on account of his wealth and position.

A second flash of light showed there before him and all else was forgotten as he saw that it persisted in its uncanny swelling brilliance. He increased the generation of theta rays and watched breathlessly as a twin star was formed there in the micro-cosmos that whirled on the screen. They fused together then, those two newly born atoms, joining forces in a violent accession of energy.

"The theta ray should be further concentrated," a cool, crisp voice spoke at his elbow.

He had not noticed the girl's presence in the laboratory, so engrossed was he in the miracle that was taking place within the tiny capsule of hydrogen.

"Yes, close to iota intensity," he replied in professional tones. "I believe that is what Gail said."

"That's right." The girl refocused the view on the screen as he adjusted the ray generator. She was an ideal assistant.

The magnification now was less than a million diameters, and still the man-made energy center was brilliantly visible and growing larger. It was taking on mass with the capture of new electrons.

"You have the primary screen?" the girl asked.

"Over there, with the small crucible he left here last night." Scott drew in a quick breath as the energy burst forth with trebled vigor, and his fingers trembled on the control of the ray generator.

"We'll need it shortly," the girl said, returning with a shiny cylinder, which she placed, beside him.

"And the secondary screens? They are in the laboratory of the fifty-third level?" he asked.

"Yes. In the keeping of the Council of Five. I'll go for them whenever you are ready."

"You have notified the Council, I presume. Gail said you were to do so." Scott slipped the primary screen in over his hydrogen capsule, and the radiation of the energy-center was dimmed momentarily to a dull, sputtering red.

"I have, and they approve of what we are doing," the girl replied. She was busy with the calculating machine, determining the rate of mass increase of the energy center.

"Then why can't they send those secondary screens up here?" Scott asked gruffly.

"Sarovin's crowd has spies watching them. It would be too risky."

"How about the risk to yourself in going down there?"

"No risk at all," the girl sniffed. "I can twist them around my finger, any of them."

Scott was not so sure; they were a desperate bunch, these who had been followers of the defunct agitator, and would stop at nothing now. Especially if Crawford had started something.

A rapid flare-up of the energy center made haste imperative. He cut back slightly into the theta ray band. "Can't be helped, I guess," he growled. "You'd better go now, Miss Rosov. Be careful, though."

"Of course." She slipped a sheet of calculations into his hand and was gone by way of the secret lift.

Remarkable girl, that. Scott checked her figures rapidly and found they were correct. It was incredible that the rate of energy increase should have reached so enormous a value. Why, in less than an hour they'd be radiating sufficient power to operate the entire pneumatic tube system of the city! If it could be used.

The energy center was visible now with not more than a thousand diameters of magnification. He slipped the cylindrical screen and its precious contents out of the microscope and transferred it to the wave reflector of his spectrometer.

For the first time he gave attention to the imperative call of the visiphone. Its buzzer had shrilled for many minutes unnoticed. Matt Crawford probably—in person. He reached for the activating lever, then changed his mind and rang for his head caretaker instead.

"Wilson," he said when the man came in, "take this call on the library extension, and, if it's Matt Crawford, tell him I can't be interrupted. I'll not talk to him."

"Yes, sir, very well, sir." Wilson backed out with horrified amazement written large on his wrinkled countenance. The master must be out of his mind, snubbing the kilowatt king; bringing the crippled radical from the fighting in the sub-levels. And the girl! But he hastened to do as he was bidden.

THE spectrometer readings showed that the radiations of the energy center held steady within a fraction of one per cent of the frequency selected from the cosmic rays by the globes of the Power Syndicate.

He returned the screened capsule to the stream of exciting rays and saw immediately that the energy center was now visible without the aid of the super-microscope. It was a pulsating pinpoint of light, the germ of a latent energy that would become so enormous in potentiality that cold calculation of the values was staggering to contemplate.

The open panel of the secret lift reminded him that the girl had been away for a much longer time than the trip should have required. A cold fear gripped him as the vibrating energy within that tiny screen sent forth an audible note. If those devils down there had harmed a hair of her head, he'd rend the sub-levels asunder with an atomic blast that would be heard around the world!

"Mr. Terris, sir, I beg pardon." Wilson stood there, pale and shaken—apologizing.

"What is it, man? Have it out."

"It—it *was* Mr. Crawford, sir, and he was furious. He said he was coming here at once, sir."

"You'll not admit him, Wilson. You understand?"

"Yes, sir. That is, no sir, I'll not." The old fellow turned trembling to leave. But he straightened his shoulders as he passed through the door and Scott knew that the main entrance to the apartment would remain bolted.

The hydrogen capsule had vanished utterly and the energy center now hung suspended and enormously enlarged in the hollow cylindrical screen. A sputtering light-ball of the size of a food pellet, it cast a circle of such intense brilliance on the metal ceiling that the sun glow illumination was dim by comparison. Alternately expanding and contracting like a living, breathing thing, it was radiating thousands of horsepowers of energy into space even now.

And still Norine had not returned. Where could she be? Scott cut back still further on the theta rays and strode to the open panel of the secret shaft, where he listened anxiously for the lift. But all was silence in the blackness down there. He dashed from the laboratory and into the room where Destinn lay.

"Norine went for the secondary screens," he groaned, "and she's been gone for more than an hour. Tell me where to find her, Gail."

The nurse remonstrated with him for exciting her patient, but he waved her away.

"She'll be all right, Terris," the sick man said calmly. "Never fear for that girl's safety."

"But if she isn't—if something has happened to her!" Beads of perspiration glistened on Scott's brow.

But Destinn coolly ignored his excitement. "Nothing will happen," he whispered confidently. "How far have you progressed?"

"A stable energy center now glows in the primary screen. Radiations are increasing at the ninety-first power every ten seconds."

"Good Lord, Terris!" Destinn's weak voice betrayed excitement now and the nurse tried frantically to silence him. "She must return soon," he moaned, despite the woman's efforts, "else it will get beyond control. The primary screen... Terris..."

And then Gail Destinn fainted.

CHAPTER FIVE
Awakening

INSTANTLY sensing the tremendous importance of the thing Destinn had been trying to tell him, Scott made desperate efforts to revive him. If only he had told him the definite composition of the metal used in those protective secondary screens; if only he could get him to speak the few necessary words!

But it was useless. Gail Destinn had slipped into a coma from which he might not awaken for many hours, the nurse told him sternly. And, if Mr. Terris had any sense of human kindness; if he had any consideration at all for a man who was desperately ill, he would leave the sick room at once.

Scott left. He dashed into the laboratory and listened once more at the panel of the secret shaftway. But, if there was any sound of the lift rising he could not have heard it for the intense note of the raging fury within that primary screen. The thing nearly filled the tiny cylinder now, and it was bouncing about at a terrific rate.

He shut off the theta rays without result. The thing seemed to take on new energy with their cessation. Of course! Excitation had been completed; the madly whirling thing would continue now in its acquisition of mass unaided. And, if not properly screened and its vast potentiality directed into the intended channels, it would go on and on until it had destroyed New York and all of its millions—until it had destroyed the Earth itself; the solar system, perhaps.

He searched through his crucibles in a frenzy. Selecting one of pure tungsten, he placed it gingerly over the small cylinder. There was a tremendous thump that seemed to wrench the very space about him, and the crucible vanished in a puff of light that left him blinking and blinded.

"Scott—Scott Terris!" a voice sobbed then intp his consciousness. "Am I too late?"

It was Norine. His vision was clearing and he saw her swaying before him, her face marble-white and her eyes staring at some nameless horror they still beheld. In her arms was a shimmering metallic object, a hollow cone with a hinged lid on the flaring end.

"Oh, oh!" she moaned, letting the cone clatter to the floor. "It's dark down there in the sub-levels—dark. They've shut off the power, Scott, and the Ways are stopped. There's terror down there and vile murdering of innocent people. The Council…I found them wallowing in their own blood, all five. And Prouty—I killed him with my bare hands!"

She swayed toward him, and somehow Scott found her in his arms. The white gleam of her body through rents in her clothing set his blood afire and he crushed her to him. For a moment she yielded, sighing. Soft, moist lips met his own and clung passionately.

Then she had pushed him away. Her eyes blazed scornfully and the white of her neck and cheeks flared a sudden angry red.

"I'm sorry, Norine, sorry," he mumbled, reaching for the all-important secondary screen. "I was mad, I guess."

In another moment he'd have the terrific thing they had created safely controlled; the energy center, at least. The other—the feeling she had created in him—could never be quenched. He wasn't sorry; he was a man insane with the new flame that burned within him.

WILSON was there, sputtering, "Crawford, sir, Crawford—the big boy himself is at the entrance. Th—three of the red police are with him, sir. They're cutting down the door with acetylene torches."

Norine screamed, "Gail, Gail! They'll get him, Scott."

She ran from the room as Scott advanced hastily to where the ball of raw energy spun crazily within the tottering primary screen. In a daze, he fumbled with the lid of the cone.

The crash of the massive steel door out there falling inward gave warning that the time was short. Damn that lid! He couldn't open the thing. The primary screen had careened violently and threatened to spew forth its fearful content.

And then they were in the laboratory, a lieutenant of red police with two of his men. Crawford bringing up the rear; dragging Norine back into the room, the swine!

"You're under arrest, Terris!" the lieutenant snapped.

"Arrest, hell!" The lid of the cone swung back and he had the mighty energy center under control.

In after years, when he thought back on that scene, he realized he must have lost his senses completely after that. Norine, when they had released her and closed the door, stood there a cold fury. He had taken advantage of the legalized companion of another man, her eyes accused him— a man who lay helpless but a few steps away. And in that maddening gaze of hers there was unforgiving antipathy— abhorrence.

What mattered it to him now that terror stalked down there in the sub-levels? What mattered the class distinctions of modern life; the injustice? All that mattered was power— power to take and to smash; to bring the highest and the lowliest to their knees. And he, Scott Terris, was master of that power. It spun there, waiting to be used, in that unassuming cone of metal that reposed on his workbench.

"Arrest!" His maniacal laugh set the lieutenant back on his heels. Terris, the mild-mannered scientist, had gone crazy!

"Drop it!" Scott yelled, as the officer reached for his riot pistol. "Drop it, I say!" He grabbed the cone, and the angry hum that arose from within silenced even the babblings of Crawford.

He snapped back the lid and withdrew the cone with a flipping motion, leaving the mysterious roaring thing it had contained to spin there in mid-air a blinding ball of fire. Fully an inch in diameter now, its note rose to a scream as it took on additional mass by the acquisition of new electrons from the disintegrated components of the surrounding atmosphere. The metal walls, the floor and ceiling of the great room emitted fearful sounds of harmonic vibration that added to the din.

Crawford, his flabby jowls sagging, opened his thick lips to cry out, but no sound came from the vocal chords that were paralyzed with fear. The lieutenant struck out at the whirling thing with the butt of his pistol. There was a thumping wrench of surrounding space and the weapon was dissolved in one of those blinding light flashes, only to add further to the mass of the dancing horror that spun so swiftly before him. Screaming, he fell back waving the cauterized stump of his forearm, from which hand and wrist had vanished.

"Power! Power!" Scott yelled, advancing on Crawford. "I'll show you what power is. Arrest me, will you? Crawford, you're through; your reign is over. I shall be Dictator in United North America. Come here!"

"YOU—can't do this, Terris," the man faltered, extending a pudgy hand before his face in feeble attempt to shield it from the searing radiations of that incredible whirling thing which had struck terror to his craven soul.

"Can't I? You haven't seen the half of what I can do. Call off your men, Crawford... You withdraw your charges, don't you?"

"W—what do you intend to do?"

"All in good time. Call them off, I say!" Scott brought the open end of the cone close to the screaming energy center and the thing drifted several feet nearer the erstwhile king of the kilowatts.

Dripping agonized perspiration, the terrified financier waved the police away. Only too glad to escape the awful menace of the thing that danced there blinding them and causing their very blood to boil in their veins, they slunk off, supporting the collapsed and moaning lieutenant between them.

Scott brought the insulating cone down over the energy center and returned it to the workbench. "That, Crawford," he said grimly, in the deathly silence that followed, "is the secret of your downfall. A man-made thing that will revolutionize the production of power and render useless all of your vast plant units out there in the stratosphere."

"You're bluffing," with a trace of his usual courage returning. "It's a laboratory trick of yours, designed to frighten us." Crawford mopped his brow nervously and straightened his slumped shoulders.

"Frightened you, too, didn't it?" Scott grinned. "No, it's not a bluff; it's the real thing. Observe the readings of the spectrometer, Crawford, and the radiation meter. Here, make it snappy!"

Cowed anew and paling visibly when Scott's fingers strayed toward the cone, he bent over the instruments indicated. The sheaf of calculations fluttered in his nerveless grip as he examined the figures that spelled the ruin of his vast enterprises, the collapse of the mighty organization he had built up.

"What do you want me to do?" he asked abjectly.

"First of all, you will obtain visiphone connection with the executive chambers in Washington—using my instrument here. You will present me to the President as your successor. Following that, you will call together the dummies who are supposed to be the directors of the Power Syndicate. You will resign as President and Chairman of the Board, appointing me to succeed you in those positions."

"But my stock, Terris—I own controlling interest."

"Bah! It'll not be worth the paper it's engraved on when I've finished. After you have done the things I've mentioned, you will establish connections with your representatives in each of the cities of our country; you will resign from each and every industrial board of which you are a member; you will transfer your proxies to me. And you will notify your spies and your undercover men in the various departments of the government of the new order of things. Get busy now, Crawford."

"Terris, the thing's impossible," the broken man pleaded. "I just can't do it—I can't!"

Scott looked at his pocket chronometer. "Crawford," he said in brittle tones, "if you're not at the visiphone in sixty seconds, making that first call, your worthless carcass will go to swell the mass of the energy center. I mean it. This power is mine; I'm taking it, and a piffling thing like the life of a man like you will not stand in my way. Step now!"

Matt Crawford moved with ludicrous haste. His fat fingers fumbled with the visiphone lever and he put in the call for President Owens.

Scott turned slowly to face Norine Rosov. The girl had stood there a rigid and scornful figure throughout the proceedings; now her pale lips moved in low, tense monosyllables.

"Thief! Cad!" she whispered huskily. "Oh, you—you—"

"Norine," he interrupted her, and his voice was silky and even. "I don't expect that you'll understand. Women never do. But this thing I'm doing is the only thing possible under the circumstances. And don't think I'll weaken in my purpose. I shall do exactly as I have said, and tomorrow the cities of United North America will have their first taste of the medicine I shall prescribe."

His jaw set in taut lines as the girl flushed in swift anger. She crouched there, braced against the wall as if about to spring upon him clawing and tearing like some wild creature of the jungle.

His next words were clipped off in steely determination. "But one thing I ask—no, I command it. You will leave Gail with me so that he can be properly treated. I give you my word he will be provided with all the attention that money can buy—the finest medical care—everything."

The fierce look of a beautiful animal went suddenly from her face and her lips trembled. "You—you promise?" she faltered.

"Solemnly."

"Yes...yes, it is better so. I couldn't provide for him," she agreed, her voice choking. "And, Scott, may I...visit him?"

"Certainly."

Crawford was talking rapidly before the disc of the visiphone where President Owens regarded him with open-mouthed astonishment.

Deliberately cruel, Scott snarled at the girl, "Go...now! Can't you see that you're in the way? *Go!*"

And Norine Rosov, beaten and sobbing, made her uncertain way to the secret lift.

CHAPTER SIX
The Old Order Changes

WITHIN two hours Scott Terris sat facing the President in the secret room of the executive chambers in Washington. He had laid down the law in no uncertain words and was regarding through eyes that were narrowed to slits, the vacillating politician who had been the catspaw of the old money-oiled machine.

Matt Crawford had departed without baggage on an extended tour of the pleasure cities of southern Europe. His letter of credit, though more limited than he would have wished, bore the official seal of the government of United North America. It was his decree of banishment.

"But, Terris," the President remonstrated mildly. "What you are doing is the acme of high-handedness. This is a republic; the people will not stand for it."

"Tommyrot! We haven't been a republic, excepting in name, for more than a century, and you know it. The people will stand for anything, provided they are moderately prosperous. They believe they would like to rule themselves, but they're incapable—they've proved it time and again all through our history and the history of the rest of the world. The best form of government for them is an absolute monarchy, and that is what we will now become. I am the absolute monarch, though I shall assume no title as such, and my word is to be the law of the land as truly as was that of the czars and emperors of old. You understand?"

President Owens dropped his tired old eyes before the flinty orbs that bored into his very soul. "You'll do nothing rash, I hope?" he quavered, glad in his heart that a strong man was taking the reins.

"Nothing at all; excepting to turn the entire country topsy-turvy and reorganize society and industry. Nothing rash, I assure you."

"Good Lord!" the President gasped.

"You haven't heard anything yet," Scott grinned. "Listen—"

He talked for more than an hour, rapidly and forcefully, and when he finished, it seemed that the President had shed twenty years of his age. There was a healthier color in his gaunt cheeks and smile wrinkles appeared at the corners of his eyes.

"Terris," he beamed. "The thing will work. I know it will work. And, six months hence, our country will be envied by the entire world. I'll call the extra session of Congress immediately."

"Oh, *that* formality," Scott sniffed. "After the newscast speech, Mr. President, after that has had time to sink in."

"Yes, yes." President Owens fluttered about, adjusting his cravat and smoothing his hair, for all the world like a little old lady preening and primping for a Sunday stroll in the ozone promenade.

For the first time during his two terms of office he was about to make a speech that would add to his self-respect. Under the magic of Scott's persuasion he had completely forgotten that he was still no more than the mouthpiece of another and greater man.

AFTER giving his orders to the Newscasting Corporation heads, Scott Terris retired to the room he had chosen for his own in the huge executive suite. The ether would be entirely cleared of traffic on the newscast wave band so that all public and private visiphones must respond to the special message of the President.

He then cut his own instrument in on the private band of the police network, calling an immediate visiphone conference of the Chiefs of Police in all cities. There was other and less public instruction to be given, and this he would take care of personally.

One by one the department heads reported in until all eight faced him in the bright disc. Merkel, of New York, he knew personally, but all of the others were strangers to him. He had greeted each in turn with a curt nod, noting with satisfaction that their bearing was subservient and respectful. The word had gone out through the secret agents of the machine and they had accepted the new Dictator without cavil. Power! He knew the secret of it, at last.

"Men," he said, "you know who I am and what has happened, so I will eliminate all preliminaries. It is sufficient for the present that you understand that all orders as to the policies and activities of the red police will come from me. I am open to suggestion, but when I have made a decision it is final—there is no appeal. Is this clear to all of you?"

He watched them keenly as they replied in the affirmative, some with quick eagerness as welcoming the change, others dubious and hesitant, yet not daring to dissent.

"Fine," he went on. "And now for the first general order. You will immediately re-allocate your men so that the upper levels are as fully patrolled in accordance with the density of population as the sub-levels. From this time forth, you are not to discriminate one whit between those of the purple and those who wear the gray. One is as liable to arrest and punishment as the other, for the slightest infraction of the law. Starting at once, and during the next twenty-four hours, all furloughs are canceled. Reserves are to be concentrated in the public squares and along the Ways to break up any and all disturbances that may follow upon the President's speech. And—get this—you are to arrest all agitators and objectors, regardless of class, and mobilize them on the roof surfaces for immediate transportation to the space globes of the Power Syndicate, where they will be sentenced to labor for an indefinite period of time—without bail. That is all for the present; good day, gentlemen."

"But, Mr. Terris," expostulated Shapley of San Francisco, "there will be trouble."

"Hmmm, a police chief worried about trouble! Of course there'll be trouble—and plenty of it. That's your job, Shapley, to face trouble and fight it."

He flicked the lever and the disc went blank. That preliminary was over, and Scott had not the slightest doubt that his orders would be carried out.

A SPECIAL frequency band was assigned to him by the Radio Bureau in order to avoid interference on the newscast wave. He glanced at his watch—Owens' speech would be on the air in ten minutes.

In quick succession he obtained connections with headquarters offices of the Power Syndicate, the Food Company, and the Air Conditioning Bureau, snapping out orders that left their officials aghast and palpitating but submissive withal. The undercover men must have done their work well, spreading the reputation of this new Dictator as a hellraiser. Scott permitted himself a sardonic smile.

He had his first assistant, Warren, on the air then and promoted that amazed individual to his old position as chief of the Research Bureau. Before the man could stammer his thanks, he was instructing him minutely in the matter of the energy center, which was to be duplicated in huge quantities at once, including spectroscopic analyses of the primary and secondary screens so that their materials might be reproduced, and plans for the projectors in which the new energy source was to be used. Power! His very words vibrated with it. Warren, a clever lad and ambitious, was quick to absorb the astounding knowledge that was imparted so unexpectedly and swiftly by his superior. Again Scott was confident of the results—they would be more than satisfactory. Warren was one chap who would get ahead.

Biting the end from his first cigar that day, he settled back comfortably to listen to the message that would create such a turmoil that the customary labor troubles, even the more serious recent ones, would pale into insignificance in the annals of the country.

He observed that the President was speaking with confidence and that his entire bearing was that of a man who believed in his subject. Power! Something of its meaning had taken hold of the little man. He positively radiated it.

The "Ladies and Gentlemen" part was over with and Owens' eyes sparkled as he got at the meat of the thing. "We are about to embark on an experiment, a most noble one," he stated crisply; "an experiment that will not meet with approval on all sides. Yet it has become a thing of grave necessity and I ask the United Americas to support the administration as it has never done before. A new era will result, an era of happiness and prosperity, I promise you, such as the world has never known."

Scott grunted. That old political ballyhoo, it would persist!

But the next was good: "We are changing our entire social and economic structure, let the axe fall where it may. For centuries we have functioned on a basis that was entirely wrong, a basis where wealth and influence determined a man's status regardless of his real worth as a member of society. All that is to be changed; beginning this day, the government will confiscate all wealth, all individual and corporate holdings, this wealth to be controlled and redistributed by a new Department of Finance that will be headed by Scott Terris, former chief of the Science Research Bureau. All wage scales are to be readjusted in accordance with the real value of the individual in the economic scheme, the individual ratings to be determined by the Boards of Education and Industrial Training in the various centers. No man or woman, from this day on, will receive more or less compensation than his or her ability merits. This will result in advancement to the ambitious and able; conversely, in demotion for the indolent and inept. A grading process, as it were, that will give every individual an opportunity as great as that of his neighbor. He will have free admission to the educational and vocational institutions, and any mental or bodily deficiency that might handicap him will be cured by our great medical and surgical men, who, in these times, are balked by nothing."

The President hesitated, wetting his lips. Scott thought with a sudden pang of Gail Destinn. But he threw off the feeling; it was not to be allowed that sentiment creep in now to interfere with straight thinking. Besides, Owens was carrying on with his message:

"Every man will have his chance; no man the advantage. The day of unemployment and economic depression is past. With the elimination of concentrated wealth and the institution of the twenty-hour working week, which is likewise a part of the plan, such situations, as that now existing, will become impossible. There will be work for everyone, and all must work in order to live. The fluctuations in supply and demand will be met by reducing or increasing the labor turnout of the mechanicals, who require no compensation or food, only power to keep them alive. And power, incidentally, is to be plentiful and cheap. This, our most vital commodity, is the crux of the situation and is to undergo a radical change in its manner and cost of production. A new process, that produces energy directly from minute and inexpensive quantities of matter, has been developed by Scott Terris, who, in addition to his other duties, has taken over the leadership of the Power Syndicate from Matt Crawford, who has resigned."

Scott grinned appreciatively. Owens was doing the thing to a turn; he hadn't thought it was in the old man, after some of his weak parrot-like speeches that Crawford had inspired.

More was to follow," but the main facts had been covered. The rest was mere detail. Scott cut back to his private frequency band and requested a sound-vision flash of the Food Company Square in level fifty, New York. About time for the fireworks to begin, and somehow he felt an especial interest in the reactions of the workers in that particular gathering place.

The sound mechanism burst forth in a terrific din when the connection was established. The remainder of the President's message would go unheard by that frantic mob. In the great central rotunda, a howling, singing group milled about and voiced their jubilation with irrepressible ardor. At other points there were gatherings of angry and disgruntled workers who formed little circles around longhaired agitators who spouted invectives against the government. But the red police were on the job. They swiftly broke up such crowds, making free use of mace and riot pistols.

He looked for the place where Sarovin had died and saw that a makeshift platform had been erected over the gaping opening in the floorplates. Here was centered the most violent demonstration he had observed, hemmed in by the red police and fighting desperately against their rushing tactics. And, on that platform stood Norine Rosov—aflame with passion and shouting her defiance over the heads of her listeners.

A fervent prayer that he might not be too late escaped his lips as he cut back to the police wave band. He must get Merkel instantly. Oh God—Norine! He'd never forgive himself if they harmed her.

CHAPTER SEVEN
Progress

IN New York City, where the concentration of wealth was greatest, the President's message was at first received by the pleasure-seekers and idlers of the upper levels with languid amusement. This was only another of Crawford's clever moves to still the clamor of the gray-clad multitude and to further enrich the coffers of those of the purple, a holding out to the workers of the bait of increased compensation for increased industry and ability, when all knew that he would only squeeze and bleed them the harder under the guise of this new scheme that was designed only to deceive them into superhuman effort in his behalf. For themselves, stockholders and directors in the many corporations he controlled, there was not the slightest cause for anxiety.

But, when they discovered that their corporation credits were no longer honored in payment for commodities or service, when they learned of the issuance of new paper by the government that was known as labor credit and could only be obtained in exchange for useful productive or directive effort, such a howl was raised as to put to shame the feeble demonstrations of the sublevels. Suddenly it was brought home to them that this thing was no joke; they were virtual paupers, and might actually starve if drastic action was not taken.

In Central Square, the huge crystal-domed recreation center of the upper levels, there gathered as choice an assemblage of the *ultra-elite* as had ever congregated in a public place. In the great amphitheater, where nightly they were accustomed to parade their finery in attendance upon the performances of the opera, they collected in angry sputtering groups in the case of the younger set and in pompous sneering aloofness where those of great power and influence met.

What was particularly amazing and abhorrent to their sensibilities was the presence of the red police in unprecedented force—an unwarranted and inexcusable invasion of their privileged immunity from such interference. It was incredible that Crawford would permit this indignity to come to them. Where was Crawford, anyway? President Owens had said he resigned from the Power Syndicate in favor of this scientist, Scott Terris. Was this, after all, the truth and not a blind? What right had Terris, who had never strayed into the realm of politics and industry from his commendable research work, to take upon himself this position of authority he seemed to have usurped? They must communicate with Crawford immediately.

Someone ferreted out Arthur Mason, Crawford's close confidant and nominal President of the Water Supply Syndicate, and was forcing a way to the stage, where gray-clad employees of the Newscasting Corporation were completing the erection of one of the raucous-throated and flickering-screened apparatuses of the public information system. Another high-handed invasion of their rights!

Mason, his massive features apoplectic in hue, and his vast bulk aquiver with righteous indignation, raised a shrill voice to address them. A semblance of quiet came then in the huge gathering-place and the red police could be observed drawing in their lines. Incredible that they should be watched like the common herd in the sublevels! But Mason would be worth listening to; he would surely know something of what had really transpired—at least he might be expected to have knowledge of the whereabouts of Matt Crawford.

"Folks!" he shouted. "This is an outrage! Why—why do you know they have actually refused to recognize my enormous credit. My very household has deserted me—the servants will not accept corporation credits in payment for their service. There is not sufficient food even in the larders of Arthur Mason. Imagine it! Something must be done…"

"Yah!" a disrespectful voice sang out from the crowd. "You're not the only one, Mason. Tell us what to do if you're so smart. What about Crawford?"

"Crawford!" the great man yelled. "He's out, just as Owens said; deserted us—gone! This young whelp, Terris, has taken things in his own hands. And the government backs him up. It's a gigantic steal—robbery! We must organize and fight him in Congress."

"Congress, hell!" the same scornful voice retorted. "They passed the necessary legislation this morning. You should know how those things are forced through, Mason—you've done it enough times."

There was instant commotion in the section from which that voice had come. An exchange of quick blows and wrathful bellowings as the man was attacked by the aroused mob. A police whistle shrilled and a dozen of the red-coated minions of the law were on the spot. Maces fell resounding on unprotected skulls and the disturbers were dragged off amid the swelling protest of the astounded audience.

Mason paled visibly. This was the real thing; this Terris had laid his plans well. From some mysterious source he had support that was making him a power in the land. Raising his voice anew, Mason yelled hoarsely in a futile attempt to shout down the rising din of the chattering, milling crowd. Like animals, they were, each intent on his own problem, each fighting for his own real or fancied wrongs and jabbering of his troubles to his neighbor. A siren shrieked and the reserves rushed into the Square to quell the incipient riot.

Exactly like the rabble of the sub-levels, it was! In disgust he turned from the sight and found himself staring at a grinning workman of the Newscast crew.

"Boo!" yelled the fellow in gray, wriggling his fingers derisively at his nose. "How do you like it, you fat slob?"

Arthur Mason had never been so addressed in his life.

Shaking his fists and screeching impotent rage, he advanced on the laughing workman. The screams of women and the hoarse shouts of men battling for their lost lives of luxury rose a monstrous unthinkable babble in his ears. His world of affluence and ease was toppling there before him.

And still that workman grinned... He'd have the satisfaction, at least, of trouncing the fellow soundly. Swinging awkwardly and with stiff joints, he drove a blubbery fist into the pit of the man's stomach. That would put him in his place. But, quick as light, the slim youngster struck out, still smiling, and hard knuckles crashed home to the point of Arthur Mason's jaw.

After that there was confusion. Somehow he had slumped to the floor and an infernal hubbub surged there around him, whirling madly and interspersed with bright specks that floated and danced in the haze. A friend bent over him— Warner Merkel in the full regalia of his office.

"Help me out of this, Merks," he whirred.

But the grim face drifting there was unsympathetic. "Sorry, old man," its lips seemed to whisper, "It's no go. I have to place you under arrest."

Truly, the world had gone topsy-turvy.

EIGHT levels below, a little knot of young men and women worked swiftly at the master controls of a humming foundry section of the mechanicals. Some of them there were who wore the purple and some the gray, but they thought and planned and labored together as a unit with no hint of the old class distinction or the turmoil in the public places of the city. These workers were in harmony, believing in the ultimate success of the change that was creating such a disturbance both above and below, accepting as their due the new independence that had come to them as individuals with their classification as capable, intelligent operatives.

All around them were the soulless, brainless mechanicals, busily engaged in the tasks to which they were assigned by the operatives. Massive man-made creatures of copper and steel, which labored at furnace and forge, at press and rolling mill in fabricating the conical secondary screens for this new energy, which the Power Syndicate was to adopt.

"They're tearing things apart down in the thirties, I heard," a bright-eyed lass in gray denim remarked to the serious youth in purple, who worked at the adjoining control board. Her nimble fingers flashed over the buttons as she spoke and the quick lighting of return signals apprised her of the proper performance of the duties of the eighty mechanicals she supervised.

"Yes, and in Central Square up top," her neighbor replied. "They arrested Mason himself when he got up to speak. Crawford's old buddy, can you beat it? And a hundred others of the fools were shipped off with him to globe 819. They'll work there."

"He's a terror, this Scott Terris," said the girl in awed voice. "Did you know him?"

"Only by sight. I worked under Warren in the Research Bureau, a political appointment, you know. Got my goat, that job—nothing to do and nobody caring." The lad puckered his brow in a puzzled frown. "Funny thing, too," he said, "I used to see Terris around. He wasn't that kind. A hard worker himself, but easy on his force. Not at all the fire-eater he has turned out to be lately."

"Bet there's a woman behind it, somewhere."

"Lord no... He wouldn't look at a woman."

"Oh yeah? Neither did Napoleon."

"Anyway," the lad in purple maintained stoutly, "I'm for him. He may be tough and hard-boiled, but the way things are going now, we'll be better off. Why can't the others see it?"

"They'll come around—when they're hungry. I've been hungry and I know."

"You have? Good Lord..." The boy was silent after that.

He stole a furtive look at the girl after a while and marveled at the flush of excitement that mantled her pretty cheeks at each new move of the huge creatures she controlled. Power! That was it; she was thrilling to the sense of it that surged through her new being.

OVER across the Hudson River a gang of laborers worked swiftly with power-saw and block and tackle, clearing away a section of woodland on the Palisades to make way for one of the new projector towers of the Power Syndicate. Many of them were breathing the outside air for the first time; some had never viewed the sun save in the travelogues of the visiphone programs. All of them worked with a will.

Only one wore the purple, a man of middle age, stoop-shouldered and hollow of eye. The others had given him a wide berth from the beginning; and he seemed so out of place, resentful, rather, in the aloof manner he maintained. But, as time went on, the foreman took notice of number 91. He was a conscientious worker and minded his business, which some of the others didn't. And now he was taking on new color; his back was straightening, and the furtive look of him was leaving. Already his first sullen manner was brightening. Once he burst forth in song, a swift snatch of sonorous baritone that rose with thrilling power and clarity, then broke off short—abashed.

Tom Carey, the foreman, walked over to where number 91 was working and consulted his payroll list before addressing him.

"Your name's Cabane, isn't it?" he inquired gruffly.

Number 91 did not look up. "'Yes," he replied mumbling.

"Mine's Carey."

"I know."

Tom Carey scratched his head. Queer bird, this one. And then he remembered. "Used to sing in the opera, didn't you?" he blurted out, and then was sorry.

The man drew himself suddenly erect and fire flashed from his eye. "I was Manuel Cabane," he said proudly. And then his eyes dropped and his shoulders sagged.

"Booze, wasn't it?" Carey asked softly. He expected number 91 to turn on him then, but the man only nodded.

A moment Tom Carey stood thinking. Then, "Like your job?" he inquired. He was curious about this fellow who had been somebody.

"I love it!" Manuel Cabane threw his head back and stared out over the river to the great steel wall that gleamed over there, hiding its millions from view. "If provides an outlet for Cabane, an outlet for those feelings that smolder here..." He thumped his chest. "I had too much money," he continued, "and was a great fool. Now that this wealth that I did not know how to use has been taken from me, I shall become a new man. I shall return once more to the opera, and this time I shall have wisdom. This devil of a Terris is an angel in disguise. They are dying over there in the city, some of them, and they say he is killing them. If so, it is for the best. Iron Terris, they are calling him—the fools. He has restored the mind of Cabane, as well as of others." And then number 91 raised his voice in all its old richness and power.

Power! Hand in hand with beauty and art. Regeneration.

CHAPTER EIGHT
Two Months Have Passed

"THERE'S a thousand labor credits in it for you, Conrad."

"Yuh got the needle gun?"

"Yes—here." Peter McKay shoved the wicked little weapon over the tabletop to the low-browed individual who faced him.

"Gimme the thousand."

"When you've finished the job."

"Nothin' doin'. Pay now, or there ain't no Job."

Con Burdig, once a mighty power in New York's fast dwindling underworld, was not taking any chances. These guys up top were crooks, especially those who lost a couple of million and had to work for a living.

"All right." McKay counted out the paper and handed it over. "There'll be no slips, Conrad?"

"Naw. I get 'em when I go after 'em, Mac." Burdig rose leering exultantly as he stuffed the credits in his pocket and patted the shiny pistol affectionately. "Don't worry about me not gettin' Terris," he grinned. "I'd kill the damn slave driver just to own this gun. I'd kill him for nothin' almost—he's busted my racket wide open, the lousy robber!"

Peter McKay mused grimly when the man had gone. Set a thief to catch a thief; that was the way to rid the country of this tyrant who had risen up overnight to tear down financial structures that had been centuries in the building and to set up a new structure of his own. Lord, how he had put it over on the rabble! And, strangely, on the great majority of his own kind. Fools! Why, there were some of them who'd never done a tap and whose top-level establishments numbered a hundred or more rooms, living in one room now, and working hard. Plugging away at trades, keeping late hours in night school—doing anything to curry favor with the Classification Bureau.

Not for Peter McKay. He had managed to scrape together a few thousand labor credits by sacrificing his air-yacht and the art objects he had collected for their value but secretly snickered over. Weird things of the past centuries and ugly, he thought them.

Nina, his companion, had gotten a severance decree and tied herself to that opera singer. Good riddance! She'd always been a poor sport anyway. Always wanting to do things that were not being done by the old clique; slumming in the sub-levels, and spending his money on a gang of bums who hung around the charity centers. The oily baritone was welcome to her!

No, he was too wise to fall for this Utopia stuff; he had his few thousand and was biding his time. With Terris out of the way, other lines he had laid could be picked up. What a bombshell he had planted! Terris, the hypocrite, was the wealthiest man in the world for all his smooth talk of equitable distribution. Well, those vast holdings would be redivided in accordance with the man's own laws after that energy needle had gotten in its work.

The schemer leaned back in his chair and a satisfied smile spread over his face as he puffed luxuriously on his cigar. He, Peter McKay, would become a power in the land after that. He was as clever as the next one, and he had friends, influence. His plans could not fail. Perhaps even, he might aspire to the position of Dictator and take to himself all of the things that great power brought. Power—and greed.

ATTIRED in the serviceable khaki of a convict laborer, a heavyset man worked perspiringly diligent with cloth and metal polish on the brass rail that enclosed the high tension switching mechanisms of globe 819. His flesh hung in loose folds about the chin, due to the loss of the obesity he once had carried. He whistled as he worked, and would permit his eyes to wander occasionally to the viewing port where the Earth was visible as an enormous ball of mottled green filling the sky in its nearby majestic immensity. He sighed after each such lapse, and the cheerful whistle was stilled for a space.

One would not have recognized in this lowliest of workers the man who had been Arthur Mason but two months ago. Out here, a hundred miles from the surface, where the great sphere drifted under gravity control that kept it at a constant distance and angle over New York, things were vastly different. One did as he was told, and there was no shirking of duty nor talking back to superiors. But one lived; the food was the best synthetic product and was amply supplied. There was every convenience; crude and elemental, of course, where cosmetics and the luxuries of the bath were concerned, but one kept clean and comfortable, and surprisingly fit.

There had been much time in which to think, and Mason had done his share of thinking. It had brought him nowhere, it was true, but he found that he no longer thrilled to certain desires that had flamed in his spirit at first, nor was he as irked over the situation as he had been in the beginning. As a matter of fact, though he would not have admitted it, there was a satisfaction in the convict life aboard the huge transforming and radiating station of the Power Syndicate he had never before experienced. Since the first week or so, when there had been much trouble and a number of casualties in rioting of the prisoners, the life had been singularly peaceful and enlightening. Some of his fellow prisoners were mighty good company, and there were the hours of recreation and amusement; opportunities for study—all one could wish for but freedom.

Most of all he missed contact with the world. There was only one visiphone on board and this was in the Chief Engineer's office, inaccessible to the prisoners. Posted bulletins were few and far between; their information meager and carefully censored. But it was generally known that conditions were improving back home. Iron Terris was running things to suit himself and with a grip that never loosened. He was relentless and cold; a man who smashed down the old and built up the new. But it seemed that his dictatorship was meeting with growing approval.

An unusual excitement was in the conditioned air of the globe today, for a rocket ship was expected from home. Officers and engineers conversed in low tones not intended for the ears of the prisoners, but news had leaked out that globe 819 was to be relieved of its load by fifty percent and that some of the convicts would be released and returned. Speculation was rife as to who the lucky ones might be.

The call bell rang out, summoning the prisoners to the central assembly hall. Mason saw the blaze of gases as the rocket ship circled the globe, slowing down for a landing in the airlock. A flutter of anxiety came over him; it just might be that he would be one of the releases—if only he were, he'd get into things back home and use some sense about it. No reason he couldn't rate a fair classification and at least be able to get along.

Special engineers of the Power Syndicate came with their test apparatus, and a detail of the red police. They had a prisoner, a ferret-eyed, dapper youth who looked out at them and at his jailers with assumed jauntiness. They'd soon take that out of him here.

And then the warden was addressing them. He called a number—108—Mason's. The trembling man stepped forward.

"You are hereby appointed trusty, 108," the warden was saying. "This prisoner, 243, is remanded to your care. Take him and see that he is bathed and uniformed."

Mason's heart sank as he led number 243 away. No release this time! But to be made a trusty; that was something. He straightened unconsciously and his chest swelled.

"What are you in for?" he asked, when the man was dressing after his shower.

"Felonious assault, they called it."

"You tried to kill someone?"

"Yeah—Terris!"

"The Dictator—good Lord!"

The new prisoner became voluble; almost it seemed he was glad to be here. "Queer fish, this Terris," he volunteered. "I coulda' got him if I half tried. Had him covered with a needle gun and damn if he didn't talk me out of it. Made me lay down the gun—with those eyes of his. He's a tough guy, all right. Then told me there was a gang of cops watching. Showed me too. There was a dozen of 'em, spread around his apartment. Gets me why he didn't let 'em bump me off."

"Good Lord! Why did you want to kill him?"

"Guy by the name of McKay hired me."

"Peter McKay?"

"Yeah, that's him. Know what that nut done? I squealed when they got me up and that bum took cyanide when they come for him."

"No! McKay killed himself?"

"Sure. No guts; they never have any, these guys that used to be rich. No guts to face the music."

"Lord!" Arthur Mason was only able to stare at the youth, who so calmly told of his crime and so discerningly judged the man who had hired him for his dirty work.

Guts! That was what they had lacked, he and his fellows of the purple.

FOOD COMPANY SQUARE in level fifty faced its visitors with a new air of prosperity. Gone were the long lines of gray-clad mendicants who awaited the daily ration of the charity center. And gone were the thousands of loiterers and the little gathering knots where red-faced agitators had been wont to air their views. But a single guard of the red police was in sight.

Over in a corner of the vast enclosure a young man and a girl sat hand in hand on one of the benches. Dressed in the smartly tailored khaki worn now by everyone who was anyone, they were a handsome couple and obviously very much in love. That they were newly mated was evidenced no more by the slender bracelet of the legalized companion that encircled the girl's firm rounded arm than by the adoration with which the lad at her side regarded her.

"Happy, kid?" he might have been heard to ask.

"You bet."

"Not sorry—for anything?"

"I should say not. Mother was furious at first. She had the old-fashioned idea that every man who wore the purple ever in his life was a scoundrel and a deceiver of women. But she knows better now. I'm afraid she's a little in love with you herself."

The boy laughed and squeezed her arm. "Honestly?" he asked. "Was that the opinion down here—before? Were we painted as black as all that?"

"Blacker. Why, a girl of the gray who would associate with one of the purple was done for; thrown out of home and ostracized by her friends. She'd have to go bad after that, or become a servant."

"Gosh…" The boy was silent for a time. "Then I sure was in luck," he whispered then.

"Silly…I'm the lucky one."

More silence, broken only by the gentle throb of the city's life and the occasional swishing rush of a pneumatic tube car beneath their feet. An incongruous figure came into view, an uncommonly beautiful girl whose close-cropped golden hair attracted instant attention as did the rather shabby gray denim in which she had clothed her magnificent figure. She walked directly to the small platform alongside the now silent newscast station and mounted it with slow steps.

"Look!" said the man. "There's that girl again."

"Yes. She comes here every night at this time. Funny about her too, Fred. I heard she has a fine position in the Air Conditioning Service; classified high in science. She's a research engineer."

"I know it. Warren told me. And yet she dresses up in the old gray every evening and comes down here to try and get an audience who will listen—to her ravings against Terris."

"Wonder why she's so rabid. She's better off than she ever was; and who cares whether he stole this energy idea of his? Fellow by the name of Destinn, isn't it, she says he robbed?"

"Yes. I never heard of him."

"Neither did I. Probably an assistant in the Research Bureau when Terris was chief. But, what's the diff? They always took the credit for inventions of their men in those days."

"Why not? Nobody recognized what a man was really worth then. It would be another matter now."

The slender figure on the platform stood there uncertainly as if waiting. Now and again the girl made as if to raise her voice, but each time thought better of it. There was no one to listen. The only ones within earshot were the young couple on the bench and they were too obviously engrossed in each other to pay attention if she spoke.

"It's odd the police never bother her," whispered the girl on the bench. "Even in the beginning, before the rioting was over, they let her talk as much as she pleased."

"Probably someone higher up is protecting her. She's harmless, anyway. What do you say, honey, wanna go home?"

"Let's do. I want to hear Cabane; he's on the visi tonight for the first time since his comeback."

Like two happy children they rose and scampered off along the path to the moving ways.

Norine Rosov stood proudly erect on the platform. With the running off of the young lovers went her last hope. What a fool she had been! Suddenly her cheeks flared an angry red.

Alone and unheeded she had fought for Gail. Battling a power that was impregnable and invincible. And to what end? Nothing she could do or that anyone else could do would make Gail happier, and no power on earth was able to do more for him than was being done.

That much she conceded to Scott Terris; he had kept his word with regard to the care of the helpless man who had discovered the energy center. But the fame and the power were Scott's, while Gail lay there unheralded and unknown. It wasn't fair!

She had kept things from the sick man on her frequent visits; told him only that which she thought would not upset him. She'd go—now—and tell him everything; how Terris had robbed him…how…

Swift feet and a turmoil of emotions carried her on the way to the secret lift.

CHAPTER NINE
Changeover

ON the seventy-fifth day following the President's message the new energy projectors of the Power Syndicate were pronounced ready for the changeover from cosmic ray power. Twelve steel towers with their titanic energy charges surrounded each of the eight great cities, ready to radiate power that would replace that of the twelve hundred globes out there in the stratosphere.

The entire cost of the project was scarcely greater than that of one of the huge globes, and there being no necessity for attendance at the projectors, one hundred and twenty thousand men and women were to be released from their duties aloft to more pleasant tasks at home. Electric power, the most essential of all the requirements of modern civilization, was to be produced henceforth for less than five percent of its former cost. Due to the savings effected in reorganization of the industry, the cost to the consumer was to be reduced in still greater proportion.

And the vast investment in the globes was not to be wasted, for they were to be returned to Earth and their materials and machinery used in the construction of the ninth city already being planned to relieve congestion, which even with the subdividing of the large apartments of the former wearers of the purple, was acute.

A new era was about to be ushered into being and Scott Terris was at the main control switchboard in Washington in person. His hand was to throw the lever that would set into motion the automatic switches and relays that would provide for the progressive withdrawing of the secondary screens that surrounded the new energy centers. And with him was the President, the members of the new Cabinet, and many prominent personages of the new regime. It was a momentous occasion.

At the main control panel of the vast system of receiving screens that spread over the roof surface of New York a network of gleaming metallic filaments, sat Ralph Warren, chief of the Science Research Bureau. Members of his staff and heads of the several departments of the city administration were grouped around him before the disc of the visiphone where was pictured the scene in Washington.

"Terris looks tired," whispered Warner Merkel, who stood at his elbow. "The job is telling on him."

"I don't think it's the job, Merks," Warren returned gravely. "Something else is eating him. He's been up to some secret experimenting with a new air yacht he had constructed. Been coming over to New York every night and hiding himself in his hangar on the west roof stage; working all night sometimes. And he's been asking me for the craziest things. He has installed a small energy projector on the ship, I am certain, and a lot of experimental apparatus. Something has gone wrong there quite recently and he's been as uncommunicative as the devil."

"Hmmm." Chief Merkel had some ideas of his own on the subject but dared not voice them. He thought he knew more about what was wrong with Iron Terris than did Warren, but he wasn't certain at all. Some hidden weakness of the Dictator would crop out sooner or later, perhaps. It hadn't been evidenced as yet, that was sure.

"Look!" Warren exclaimed. "He has thrown the switch." All eyes turned to the huge panel, when one hundred and fifty small indicating lamps glowed brightly, each showing that one of New York's power supply globes was in operation.

A group of the lamps dimmed slowly and flickered out. The master wattmeter showed no change in the total city load. But more than ten million kilowatts had been transferred from the old supply source to the new. They saw Terris smile as the frequency meter showed not a flicker of variation.

All over the country the same thing was happening; without a hitch or a single interruption of the flow of power the great changeover went forward. Within the hour more than two billion kilowatts, roughly three billion horsepower would have been transferred to the new system.

"817, 818, 819, 820," an assistant intoned as others of the lamps flickered out on the New York panel.

"Arthur Mason is on globe 819," Merkel remarked. "I got his release order from Washington only this morning."

"Is he classified?" young Warren asked, his eyes glued to the face of the master wattmeter.

"No, but there have been good reports on him from out there. He is to report personally to Terris."

Ralph Warren whistled. "That's unusual, isn't it, Merks?"

"First time it's happened."

There was silence then in the control room, save for the clicking of relays and the calling off of globe numbers by the assistant.

"Say!" Merkel hissed as the thought struck him, "I wonder what's become of Matt Crawford? There hasn't been a word about him since he left. And Matt wasn't one to give up without a struggle."

Warren stared. That was certainly food for thought. He'd like mention it to Terris next time he saw him, but he'd not dare. No one dared approach him on a subject like that.

Later that same day, Iron Terris made his first appearance before the public, speaking briefly over the newscast system. And all over the land the people in their homes and at their tasks, in the public squares and ways, turned eyes and ears to the visiphone. Not one who had reached the age of reason would have missed the event; they waited with bated breath for the stern lips to open.

When he spoke it was with a smile, and it was afterwards said by many that the smile came as a benediction, by others that it was a satiric and sneering thing that belied the worded intent of his speech. But all were in agreement as to the greatness of the man. In more than two centuries, the students of history said, there had not been a greater person in American public life and politics.

They had not expected him to speak as he did, simply and humbly in his sincerity, yet with a hint of the inward strength that had given him the mighty power he wielded.

"Citizens," he had said, "I come before you to tell you of what is unquestionably the greatest accomplishment of modern times. We have succeeded in harnessing some of the energy of the atom to turn the wheels of industry, to light our cities and purify the water we drink and the air we breathe. Many changes have preceded the accomplishment between the time of its inception and of its completion; more will follow. And you will agree, I am sure, that the trend of these changes has been and is toward the greatest betterment of the lives of the greatest number of our people. This new power, which will come to you plentifully and cheaply, is the thing that has brought about all of these changes, and it is a thing for which we are indebted to a man of whom little or nothing is known. The man of whom I speak discovered the basic principle that has been used in the development, and in his efforts was so unfortunate as to meet with an accident that has made him a life-long invalid, helpless and uncomplaining.

"This man's name is Gail Destinn. Probably not a hundred of you who are living today know who this man is, or care. Nevertheless, he is our greatest benefactor and we are honoring him by christening the new energy with his name. No longer will you hear of the Power Syndicate, but of Destinn Power, as the cooperative organization, which has risen from the ashes of the old syndicate. It will be known by that name in the future. In addition to this, the Department of Finance has today conferred upon the inventor a life income of ten thousand credits a month. My only wish otherwise in furtherance of his welfare is that his lost health might be restored, so that he might take over the position now held by me as head of the great industry that will bear his name.

"That wish being impossible of fulfillment, I must carry on in the work. However—and I leave you with this thought—Gail Destinn must receive his full measure of reward, either in this world or elsewhere. Many of us in these days give little thought to the personal Deity whose name we take in vain, or to the after life that was so real an expectation to our remote ancestors. But, as surely as I stand here facing you, there is a Higher Power we do not understand and can never hope to approach. Whatever that Power is, it is something that takes the souls of men and lifts them to the heights or lets go and allows them to fall to the depths. And it is to such a Power that I ask you to send prayers for the soul of Gail Destinn. Farewell, citizens, and may you prosper and gain happiness in the new order of things."

That was all, yet it left the hearers prey to emotions they had not experienced in their lifetimes—and uncertainties that confused them and left them to wonder as to the manner of man who had spoken.

WHEN darkness had come to the East Coast cities, Scott Terris arrived in New York on one of the fast inter-city liners. Several of the "800" globes already had drifted in from the positions they had maintained in the stratosphere for periods of time up to a half century. They lay, great dark mounds over against the skyline in the forests on the Jersey side, their outlines vast blurs in the hazy night and the many-lighted ports gleaming tiny blue-white dots in the gloom.

But Scott gave little thought to the unusual beauty of the sight, nor heeded the spell of the night. His mind was too filled, and his heart, with memories of that moment of tempestuous passion when Norine Rosov had melted into his embrace as if she belonged there and would forever remain. The lawful companion of another man, yet belonging to him in that swift yielding as surely as was he certain that the flame had burned itself out in that one mad instant of hers and left her despising him and herself for the lapse.

He had power that would enable him to take anything save the one thing he wanted most of all. He had ridden roughshod and unfeeling over others who had stood in his way, but to do the one thing that might enable him to take her was impossible—unthinkable.

Possessed of the opportunity to make happiness possible for others, he was utterly helpless to provide it for himself.

But he would visit Destinn this very night; advise him in person of the success of the new energy and of the recognition he had been given. That much he could do for the poor devil, at least. He had not seen him in weeks and rather looked forward to the meeting, hoping yet fearing he might find Norine at the bedside. The sight of the girl, hating him as she did, would bring intense pain, but there would be pleasure in that pain...the chance to drink in her unattainable loveliness and to think...of what might have been...

Wilson beamed when he admitted him to the apartment that now was maintained solely for the comfort of Gail Destinn. The old fellow had become the proudest servitor of the upper level since his master came to be so eminent a personage.

"H'lo Wilson," Scott greeted him brusquely. "How's the patient?"

The old man's face fell. "Not so well, sir, I fear," he said.

"What? Why, Mowry has been reporting satisfactory progress."

"Yes sir, begging your pardon, sir," Wilson quavered. "But Miss Norine was here about two weeks ago and it seems she excited him unduly. He has been sinking ever since, the nurse tells me."

"Norine has not seen him in two weeks?"

"No sir. And it's odd, sir; she came frequently before."

"I know." Scott was filled with strange foreboding; come to think of it, he had had no reports from his agents on the girl in about that length of time. He stepped into the sickroom.

Gail lay there immobile and with eyes closed as when he had last seen him. Almost one would have thought that life had left the stricken body, so white was the man and so utterly inert.

The nurse warned him with a quick gesture. "He's sleeping, Mr. Terris," she said, "and must not be awakened. The least excitement would be certain to cause his death."

Scott looked down at the man whose once virile features were so pinched and still. Certainly his life hung by a thread. What if he were to awaken him and shout out his love for Norine? The nurse had said that any excitement...? And with the power that now was his, no man would be the wiser...*she* could be silenced—the nurse...and there would be Norine. He'd take her, whether or no.

Great beads of cold perspiration stood out on his brow as the battle raged furiously within. The man was completely in his power—and the girl who had been his mate. So simple, the thing would be. He groaned in agony of spirit and breathed a silent plea for strength to that Power he had spoken of in the afternoon.

Turning then with sudden decision he beckoned the nurse into the corridor. "What's all this?" he hissed. "Tell me what's wrong." He trembled as with the ague from the stress of emotion that had torn him. But he had himself under control; his senses had returned.

The nurse paled. "It's really not for me to say, sir," she whispered—nervously.

"You know?" he snapped, eyeing her keenly.

"Y—yes, but I dare not tell. Please don't ask me to, sir."

"I command it!" Afraid of her job, just as in the old days, he realized. These damned ethics of the medical profession, how they did hold on in spite of everything.

"You—you'll protect me with the registrar?"

"Of course," impatiently. "Out with it, nurse."

"It—it's Doctor Mowry. Oh, I shouldn't be telling you, but he is not all that he has been considered. In fact, he's been derated by the Medical Classification Board. And, his treatment has been all wrong. Oh, it's terrible, Mr. Terris—Destinn is dying, when he might well have been saved." The woman wrung her hands in agitation.

What was this? The great Mowry not what he had been cracked up to be? And here Scott had thought Gail was getting the best there was in attention, when actually he was being neglected. The devil take Mowry! Perhaps wrong in his first diagnosis; poor old Destinn might have been made well and strong—in proper hands.

He rushed to the library and bellowed hoarsely into the visiphone for the wave channel of the Medical Center. Doctor Travis and young Bedworth—the best there were—he'd have them all in consultation. Right here, in his own apartment, without delay!

A half-hour later he hunched nerveless in his chair from the reaction. Yes, Travis would operate. It was a delicate adjustment, but there was every chance that Destinn would be restored to normal health and strength. A miracle, almost!

And to think he had been on the point of causing Gail's death! To have considered it even for a moment was horrible—horrible.

Scott Terris shuddered.

CHAPTER TEN
Ultimatum

THE visiphone broke in on his thoughts with its shrill clamor. It was Warner Merkel. What could he be wanting at this hour?

"Sorry to bother you," the Police Chief apologized, "but you asked me to notify you immediately when Arthur Mason reported with his release. Mason is here, Mr. Terris."

Might as well see Mason at once. It would be something to occupy his mind while he awaited the report from Travis on the operation.

"Good," he returned. "Bring him right over, Merkel."

Excellent reports he had had on Mason. Most surprising of any of the cases of individual adaptation to extreme reverses that had come to his attention. A model prisoner, he had applied himself to his duties and to self-imposed studies with the enthusiasm of a schoolboy. Worked himself to the position of trusty; then covered himself with glory by saving the warden's life from that same young maniac whom McKay had hired to assassinate Scott. Actually broke the fellow's neck with his hands when he dragged him from the strangle hold he had on the warden. Stout fellow, Mason. He'd have to do something for him; perhaps he might give him a little the better in classification by attending to it personally.

Thirty pounds lighter and looking fifteen years younger, Arthur Mason came to him as a distinct surprise even when he fully considered his record. It was an astounding transformation.

"Any hard feelings, Mason?" he asked, when Merkel brought him in.

"None." The man faced him with sparkling eyes. "I have only thanks to give you, Terris, for what this thing has done for me and mine—and for millions of others."

"Your son, too?"

"Surest thing, you know. Fred wasn't worth a whoop in the job I wangled out of you for him in the Research Bureau. They classified him in the mechanical controls and he's making good; a foreman already. And, would you believe it, he has mated up with a wonderful girl and settled down. A little black-eyed thing who thinks he's a god and is as clever and pretty as she can be. They met me at headquarters when I came in. Imagine this, Terris, her father was a worthless scamp, one of those who never would work and always yelled his head off about conditions. A professional dissenter. Got mauled fierce in the early uprisings and finally went to work in the pneumatic tube service—best he could do. But the girl worked herself up out of it to the same sort of job Fred's first classification set him at. She came up and he down—to meet. And now they're working up together."

This was the sort of thing that renewed Scott's belief in the thing he had done. Sometimes he was aghast at the bloodshed and the privation of those first mad days, but a case like this brought new faith and a warm glow of satisfaction.

"That's great, Mason," he grinned. "And now, how about yourself? Where would you like to be classified?"

The man drew himself up proudly. "I'm willing to take my chance with the others," he averred. "Whatever classification the Board sees fit to give me is the one I want. And I'll make good, Terris."

Merkel smiled broadly and winked at Scott. Here was something with which to silence the objectors, and a man who could do it, if given the chance.

"We'll see, Arthur, we'll see," Scott said absently. The call of the visiphone had rung out and he reached quickly for the lever. Must be Travis, to tell him of Gail's chances.

But the face that appeared in the disc was not the doctor's. It came as a shock, that countenance imaged there a distorted and fear-ridden thing. Carpenter, President Owen's private secretary, it was.

"You!" Scott gasped. "Speak up, man, what is it?"

"The President, Mr. Terris! He's been killed, and the executive chambers are in ruin. Bombs, sir, from the air."

A brilliant flash then and a deafening roar as Carpenter's agonized face was blasted from the disc. The visiphone went dead.

"I KNEW it!" Terris shouted. "Bound to happen, sooner or later. Get me some volunteers, Merkel—quick! Crew for my yacht." He was half out of his robe and reaching for his khaki coat in quick energy.

"Right!" Chief Merkel put in an emergency call for headquarters. "But, Terris, good Lord! This is impossible—what the devil is it?"

"Crawford, as sure as you were born. My men lost track of him two months ago in Cannes. I've been suspicious ever since. But I hardly expected it this soon."

"But he had little means. What could he do?"

"Pirates, man. Plenty of them in the mountain vastnesses of Asia. Don't you see? He promised them the privilege of looting our cities if they'd help him take his old place here. Hell, it's as plain as day to me—but the President! I hadn't counted on that...somehow."

Merkel was speaking rapidly to his local captain, who nodded in quick understanding. "Need a pilot?" he asked, turning to Scott.

"Yes. I'll have other duties," grimly. "A good one, Merks, and three engineers."

"I can pilot your yacht," Mason broke in eagerly.

"You?" Scott saw he was white with excitement.

"Sure, I had my own license as a private owner. And, Terris, I hate to think of Matt getting away with this."

"Good stuff! Let's go…"

"Only the engineers, then?" Merkel asked, holding his connection.

"Yes. Have 'em on the west landing stage, midtown, in fifteen minutes," Terris flung back from the doorway.

And then he was gone, Mason following on his heels. Warner Merkel stared after them, thinking of his conversation with Ralph Warren that afternoon. It all fitted in to perfection—excepting the girl of the lower levels. The weakness of Iron Terris had not yet come to light; perhaps it never would.

The calamitous tidings were already on the newscasts when the two reached the pneumatic tube and were whirled rapidly downtown. Every tongue babbled of the incredible thing Crawford had done. Aligned himself with the cutthroats of the Himalayas, bringing them to prey upon the defenseless cities of America—and murdered Owens in his bed first thing! Destroyed three of the new energy towers, leaving Washington short of power; then shot skyward in the pirate vessel and calmly cut in on the visiphone system, laying down the law to the people of United North America.

Mason turned meaning eyes to Scott as a girl in the aisle of the car repeated the story of the ultimatum issued by Crawford. Good thing the Dictator was unrecognized by his fellow-passengers. There would have been a delay—possibly worse.

Crawford demanded that Terris be given up to him as the price of immunity from further attacks, the girl said. He was giving to the American people exactly one hour in which to comply with his demand and was awaiting official visiphone reply. Failing in this, they were to be subjected to a murderous bombardment of all eastern cities. The destruction of the new energy towers would leave them in utter darkness and without means of transportation while the slaughter went on. He was certain, however, that the American people were far too intelligent to refuse his demand. He fully expected them to have this tyrant Terris under guard on the roof surface of Washington well within the prescribed time. And he, Crawford, would then return to the position from which he had been ousted and they, the people, would benefit by his restoration of conditions to their former desirable state.

"Nice program," Scott muttered, "for him. If he were able to carry it out."

But the crowded car was in an uproar when they alighted at the station beneath the midtown stage. Opinion was divided and feeling ran high. Where was Terris anyway? He would be able to do something. Wasn't it better to give him up and return to the old ways than be murdered in their beds and in darkness? Mighty tough though to give up what some of them had gained. Terris was a wizard; he had the right idea of the way to run things. But he was a hard master. Enriched himself, too, while he was about this reorganization of the country. Vehemently, the lie was given to that last remark and a fight had started when the car doors were opened.

They were out then, on the great stage, he and Mason. Scott ran swiftly to where the slim tapered cylinder, which was his yacht, rested in its cradle.

"I'll see him in an hour, all right," he grated, jerking open the steel door. "But he'll not see me, Arthur. Give him a chance to let loose those devils in our cities, and to upset the work of the past eleven weeks? I think not!"

"You have weapons?" Mason inquired, when they were in the control room. "Weapons of sufficient power?"

"And then some. Look here!"

Scott uncovered a gleaming cylinder that poked its nose through the vessel's bow after the fashion of one of the ancient needle guns of the largest calibre.

The engineers trooped in then, interrupting, and Scott directed them aft. Immediately the rising whine of the main motors apprised him of their activity in the engine room. Destinn Power, radiated to the sky lanes for regular traffic requirements, was being converted to their own uses aboard. In a moment the anti-gravity force lightened the vessel and she rocked gently as she drifted from her berth. Mason grinned delightedly as he turned her nose skyward.

THE metamorphosed financier proved himself an excellent pilot and a cheerful shipmate. He pushed the vessel to her utmost in following the radio beacon lane to Washington, while Scott busied himself with the ray projector he had developed during his mysterious visits to New York. The reaction tubes astern throbbed steadily under the continuous emission of their repelling rays.

"How does that weapon work?" Mason asked.

"It's a most amazing thing, Arthur, and I actually discovered it quite by accident. Curiously, it utilizes the new energy, though the radiations have no power in themselves of destroying matter at any distance. The frequency is too great, and must be converted before we can even use it for power. But I stumbled on a principle that derives from it a most destructive force. It's quite simple, too. An energy center is at work in the tube, and its radiations are projected along a carrier beam that is of ultra-violet frequency and so adjusted as to heterodyne the Destinn wave. A harmonic of the resulting heat frequency is in the infra-red range at the most intense peak, and we thus have a formidable heat ray; a tremendous blast that will fuse even the hardest metals instantly."

"Oh, I see." Arthur Mason laughed. "For all the camouflage of big words," he said, "I take it the thing is a heat ray. That ought to be enough for me to absorb at one sitting."

"There'll be plenty for the fellow at the business end of the ray to absorb, you can bet." Scott opened the breech of the weapon and withdrew the secondary screen from a fully developed energy center, slamming the block home vigorously to confine it.

He saw Mason pale at sight of the weirdly roaring thing whose emanations set every metallic object in the control room in shrieking vibration in the brief instant of exposure. But his hands were as steady at their tasks as if nothing out of the ordinary had occurred.

Scott marveled anew at the change in the man, and at his composure in the face of the thing they had set out to do.

"You realize what this trip means, don't you, Mason?" he said, after regarding him for a moment. "You know we are going out to kill your old buddy—unless he should get us first."

"Sure, I know." Mason stared out intently through the forward port into the blackness outside. "It doesn't bother me, either, Scott. The strange thing about it is that I've practically no feeling in the matter personally. I used to eat out of his hand—before. Thought he was my best friend and I his. But something has come over me to change all that; it is as if he were a total stranger, an enemy. And he is an enemy, Scott—the worst the country has ever had. And if he gets us before we get him—which he won't—it would be an unthinkable disaster. Not for ourselves; we'd be out of it, but think what would happen down there. We've got to get him, Terris."

"Glad you feel that way."

From the tone of Mason's voice and the glitter in his eye, Scott knew well that he had a pilot in whom he could trust.

CHAPTER ELEVEN
Nemesis

"IT beats me how he got them to come over here, at that," Mason remarked, when they were within a few miles of their goal.

"Yes, though undoubtedly he promised them the world with a fence around it. And fuel for their return. They'll be heavily armed, too. These pirates have been the terror of the skylanes over there ever since the war and have taken billions in loot from the trade vessels. Thousands of lives have been lost in the many attempts to wipe out their strongholds. Their ships, you know, are converted cruisers of 2212 and they have plenty of the old armament."

"Yes. Pity our cities haven't some sort of protection."

"Oh, it was never necessary over here. The disarmament league would have allowed us such defenses as they did overseas, if we needed them. But, depending on rocket propulsion as they must, none of these pirate ships would dare make the crossing with no hope of refueling; that's why we've always been safe. But with Crawford promising them a free hand, it's different."

"Promises he couldn't keep if they did succeed," Mason grunted. "The people would never give you up to him, and even without this ship you've armed, we would drive them out eventually."

"Eventually is right. They'd smear several of our cities over the map in the meantime, though. We mustn't let them do it, Arthur."

Lightning flashes ahead revealed suddenly a bank of low-flung storm clouds and the wind-whipped waters of the

Potomac below. Mason turned the vessel's nose sharply upward. "We won't let 'em, Scott," he grated. "You do the shooting and I'll run circles around 'em with this ship." He signaled the engine room for full speed ahead.

Scott glanced at the chronometer. It lacked but seven minutes of Crawford's hour. He cut the visiphone in on the open wave band.

The storm raged furiously beneath them as they climbed higher, and the yacht bumped heavily in air pockets created by the disturbance below. It was a wild night Crawford had chosen for the attack.

Five minutes! Scott pressed the release of the heat ray to tryout his weapon. The projector tube sang spitefully clamorous and he saw the swift stabbing pencil of green that marked the path of the ray out there in the night. A harmonic in that portion of the spectrum made the beam visible. Satisfied, he peered through the gloom in the direction of the capital city.

And then the visiphone spoke. No image was pictured in the disc but a familiar voice snarled from the sound mechanism. Crawford! He was using only the voice transmitter on the pirate ship.

"THREE minutes left!" the voice snarled; "Only three minutes in which to save yourselves. I am directly above the northeast landing stage, awaiting the appearance of the upstart Terris. If he's not there on the minute, I keep my word."

"He's down there already," Scott shouted. "Hop to it, Arthur!"

The altimeter showed twelve thousand feet, and the light spot on the chart indicated their position as directly over the city. But the tossing storm clouds hid its vast area from view.

There was nothing to do but to make the dive and have it out with the pirate vessel in the midst of the tempest.

"Right-o," Mason sang out cheerily. And he put down the nose of the little ship in a power dive that carried them earthward at terrific speed.

They were in the thick of it then, flying utterly blind, the yacht buffeted and tossed so violently that the great motors aft groaned in lurching waves of sound from the gyroscopic effect. A tremendous flash lighted the control room in a glare that left them blinking and sightless as the very universe crashed in a maelstrom of earsplitting sound. It was as if they were caught helpless in the very maw of a titanic disrupting force that caved in the sides of the vessel upon them and drove their breath from their lungs in explosive blasts. The air in the control room was charged to such intensity that miniature repetitions of the lightning flash chased from deck to deck and died sputtering in the steel framework of the hull.

And then they were through; the great roof surface of the capital city lay beneath them, the edges of its towering cliffs and the landing stages lighted with the neon glow that marked them for the ships of the air. Hovering over there above the northeast stage was a huge bellied monster with a multitude of topside ports brightly lighted. It was the pirate vessel, as large as one of the transoceanic trade ships, and capable of carrying no less than three thousand fighters.

Mason pulled the little yacht out of the dive with consummate skill, his eyes popping and the veins in his temples swelled to bursting with the effort it cost him. They skimmed the roof surface and zoomed up once more in the pelting rain to get the advantage of altitude.

They had not been observed and Mason nosed the ship down to give Scott opportunity of getting the pirate vessel on his sights.

Crawford's voice snarled once more in the visiphone. "Time's up!" it announced.

On the second word a vast explosion tore away the great landing stage underneath and left a gaping opening that extended down through at least five of the upper levels. Huge girders and twisted sections of steel plate crashed down again to add to the destruction, and Scott had a momentary glimpse of bodies, ant-like and still, huddled in grotesque piles where the sun-glow of the interior filtered through the wreckage.

He pressed the release of the ray and a furrow of dazzling white cut across the stern of the pirate ship. Huge blobs of molten steel sloughed away and fell sputtering to the roof surface, which sagged and caved in under the incandescent masses.

"Hey!" Scott yelled. "This won't do. We'll have to get 'em out from over the city or we'll do as much damage down there as to them."

His words were drowned out by a terrific thunderclap that came simultaneously with a lightning flash which struck the roof and spread web-like over the surface in tiny rivulets of light that died out as they were grounded in the steel structure.

The pirate vessel lurched heavily from the sudden loss of weight astern. She canted nose down, then leveled off and sped across the city to drop a second bomb.

"Probably mistook your first shot for lightning," Mason gloated. "They haven't sighted us."

"Looks that way. But how the devil will we get them out in the open?" Scott's finger tensed on the trigger of his projector, yet he dared not pull it again. The weight of that enormous vessel crashing below would take more terrible toll than a dozen of their bombs.

And then the pirate ship turned sharply upward and hurtled off into the night. A sustained lightning flash revealed her dark bulk speeding off over the river where a second large ship drifted lazily toward the city.

"Good Lord!" Mason gasped. "The night liner from Moscow. They'll get her for sure."

Quick as a flash he was after them, and Scott sent forth the heat ray in repeated spurts that showed dazzling and dripping punctures of the pirate's hull where they contacted. But he had not reached a vital spot, for the ship of death sped on toward the ill-fated liner. Her nose spouted fire, again and again, and swift flying light-pencils darted forth to bury themselves in the curving bow of the unarmed and unprotected vessel.

"What needle guns!" Scott groaned. "Must be three inch tubes, at least. They're done for, poor devils."

The bow of the liner mushroomed in brilliant pyrotechnics now, lighting the scene with the intensity of a huge magnesium flare. A moment the great hulk hesitated, staggering, then commenced her swift wabbling dive to the river. Disintegrating before their eyes, her interior a roaring furnace, she spewed forth her passengers and crew in masses of struggling and screaming humans who hurled themselves to their death in the dark waters a half mile below rather than to face the more horrible destruction of the searing energy.

Cursing, Mason drove in toward the pirate, and the heat ray traced a wandering, deep-boring pattern on her side as Scott searched for her vitals.

A FLASHING shape rose up from the plunging liner, darting straight for the nose of the pirate. "The captain's yacht!" Scott exclaimed. "Can he be armed?" He withheld his fire as the slim shape whizzed across his sights.

"Armed? It isn't permitted," Mason grunted sarcastically. "Watch him, Scott! What in the—"

There were flashes of the pirate's big needle guns, but that tiny flitting yacht drove in unmindful of their thunderous crackling. One of the energy needles, driving down from above, carried away a section of the hull amidships and the gnat-like attacker reeled drunkenly from its course. But, doggedly persistent in his mad purpose, the captain wrenched his little vessel into the line of fire once more and flung it headlong at his monstrous enemy.

Driven nose on at fell speed, the slender steel yacht buried half its length in the control room of the pirate, smashing observation ports and tearing hull plates in the magnificent attempt of the captain to wreak some measure of vengeance for the thing that had been done.

"There's a man!" Scott yelled. "Killed himself trying to cripple them. Probably did it, too."

"No—look! They're under control." Mason swung the yacht over and into a swift spiral as the pirate turned with suddenly flaring searchlights.

In the dark waters below, the liner was settling to her last berth, a plunging mutilated monster that vanished in the steaming geyser that rose to mark the spot. And, above them in the wreckage of the tiny ship that clung welded to the pirate, her captain lay a formless pulp, his gallant life crushed out in that vain attempt to get at the murderers of those who had trusted their lives to him.

A roaring light-pencil flashed by and Mason was flung forward as the vessel careened violently into the air pocket that followed in its wake. But he clung to the controls and brought the ship over in a loop to swing in toward the monster once more.

"Not too close," Scott warned him. "I'm trying for the magazine."

The pirate had located them now and was maneuvering to get them in range of her needle guns. As if in shame before the demonstration of man-made power and ferocity below, the storm was scudding off before the wind. The lightning flashes at the horizon seemed but weak imitation of the stabbing flares that spurted from the great ship where Matt Crawford was making his last stand.

But Mason was quick as thought at the controls and the little ship fluttered and dodged in the storm of energy like a thing alive. Clinging to the projector pedestal, Scott kept his finger on the ray release as he bored relentlessly into the pirate.

A huge splash of molten metal came slithering down from the belly of the big ship and washed across the ports before his eyes, sending glass splinters flying, as the windows burst in under the intense heat. A river of the stuff washed in and spattered, the odor of scorched flesh rising in the suddenly stifling air of the control room as both Mason and he were seared.

But ever the green ray bored deeper into the vast circling bulk above them, and Arthur Mason maneuvered the little ship like a veteran dog-fighter of the old days.

Scott yelled as a shining cylinder dropped from a knob-like protuberance on the underside of the pirate vessel. Mason saw it in the same instant and yanked the yacht out from underneath as the bomb screamed past to burst in the river far beneath them and send a flaming waterspout reaching skyward.

But the green ray was bright on that protuberance now and Scott twisted rapidly at the sighting controls as he strove to hold it there. The knob glowed swiftly white and there came an explosion that lifted the great vessel like a toy and sent forth an eruption of liquid fire and hurtling wreckage that battered them down in its iron hail.

The universe was ablaze in a frightful blast that hammered at their eardrums like the crack of doom. A terrific jolt sent them reeling and clinging to the stanchions for support.

"We're hit, Scott!" Mason gasped. "Two of the motors are dead."

He was tugging at the controls then, pulling up the nose to gain altitude. The little vessel responded feebly with one third of normal power, groaning and shuddering as she climbed slowly to where the pirate hovered foundering. The great searchlights had flickered out and the needle guns ceased firing; the pirate, suddenly without power and with her midsection blown away, was poised for her last dive.

Scott switched on their own lights and they circled to the nose of the stricken vessel. Under the intense glare they could see a mass of men that huddled in the battered control room as the big ship went down by the stern.

"See if Crawford is there!" Mason hissed, following them down.

They drifted in closer until their ports were but a few feet from where those panic-stricken devils crawled around and fought and scrambled to climb through to the outer surface of the hull in forlorn hope that they might swim away from the wreck when she hit the water.

His finger tensed on the ray release, Scott looked for Crawford. Faster and faster the big ship slipped down into the blackness. Some of those who had crawled out followed the example of the victims on the liner and cast themselves from the doomed ship. Others clung to the projecting girders and flapping sections of the torn hull, fighting off those of their fellows who coveted the points of vantage.

And then Scott saw Crawford; terrified, trembling, and with great beads of perspiration glistening on his forehead, the man stared directly at him. Seeing Terris, he fell to his knees and stretched forth his hands with palms outspread as if to ward off the ray he expected would come. But that avenging beam of green light was not forthcoming; Scott could not find it within himself to press the trigger.

Suddenly the black waters were very near and Mason leveled off to turn upward. But not before they had seen an evil pirate face that grimaced horribly as it was pressed close to Crawford's. The flash of a small needle gun, and a flare within the wreck that was quenched in bright bubbles as the waters closed in over all and it was over.

CHAPTER TWELVE
Revelation

IN solemn ceremony, Washington buried its dead while the whole world buzzed of this battle in the clouds and of the triumph of Iron Terris. That Arthur Mason had piloted the tiny ship, whose mysterious ray had shot the pirate down, was a nine-day wonder. And in many sections of Asia and Central Europe officialdom breathed easier in the knowledge that the most dangerous of the several pirate bands had been exterminated. Perhaps even they might expect aid from America's Dictator in making a similar end to those who still infested the mountains.

Vice President Peterson had taken the oath of office and now was recognized as President. His succession to the title in replacement of the murdered Owens was hailed with scarcely a flutter of excitement, for the world knew that Iron Terris remained at the helm and in that knowledge was serenely confident of what the immediate future held. Terris was a young man—not yet thirty-five—and many years of his firm and sagacious guidance might be expected to work miracles for United North America and the world at large.

But Scott would have none of the adulation they tried to force upon him, for well he remembered those first frenzied weeks so short a while back, when, in open rebellion and in secret plottings, in rioting mobs and in the more sinister attempts of the would-be assassins, they had worked against him. And only too well did he know that his power over them would wane with the first sign of softening or relaxation of his iron grip. He was worn and tired and most gladly would have welcomed a release and rest, but, knowing that he must carry on in order to prevent a return to the old ways, he held himself sternly aloof and unapproachable, a mysteriously inflexible personage that was the more strongly entrenched in the popular fancy.

Confidential advice had come to him from the Medical Center in New York that Gail Destinn was fully restored to his normal capabilities by the operation Travis had performed, and was now recuperating in Scott's own apartments. Forgetting all else, he hastened to the great city that sprawled in its steel-cased irregularity of outline along the Hudson River.

For some reason, he could not have explained, he had kept Arthur Mason with him. There was a quality in the man's new character he could not define, a quality that adapted him to some particular niche where he would be most valuable to society. He had not been able to determine the location of that niche as yet and was waiting for the inspiration that would come sooner or later. Together, they made the trip on one of the fast inter-city liners.

GAIL DESTINN rose from his wheelchair with alacrity when they were admitted to the sick room. He was thin and somewhat pale as yet, but the sparkle had returned to his eyes with the ability to use his body once more. The nurse, radiantly respectful, bowed herself from the room.

"Terris," Gail said, "this is a strange reunion—for me. In the past few days I have learned the news. All of it, I think. And I don't know what to say to you; how to express my gratitude."

"There's nothing to say, Destinn," Scott returned gruffly.

"Oh, yes there is—plenty. But I can't say it properly, except this: what you've done for the country speaks for itself; what you've done for me is a debt I may never repay. And the thing you accomplished with my discovery is a miracle far beyond the wildest dreams I had entertained. No one but yourself could have put the thing across—I see it now. With my complete lack of prestige and influence, I was helpless. And the plans of the Council of Five would have gone for naught, even had they succeeded. Only in the way it was done and by the man who did it, could things have turned out as they have. I'm amazed, and—and humble, Terris. I—I—"

"That's enough, Gail. You're lying like a gentleman and entirely forgetting your part in the matter; the hard work and the vision in the research that made the whole thing possible." Scott gripped Gail's hand in sudden appreciation of the friendship that showed there in the fine eyes under that flaming thatch. He needed friends now, friends who would stick close and who would understand. "And you'll be able to take over your new duties when?" he asked.

"You mean at the head of the Power Syndicate?" I listened to the recordings of your speech, Terris. I—I can't do it. It's too big a thing."

"Nonsense! You can do anything you set out to do. And this job is yours, Gail; you are the one man for it. Not as head of the Power Syndicate—forget that old designation—but of Destinn Power."

Gail Destinn looked long and earnestly at the man they called Iron Terris. Perhaps what he said was true; perhaps he *could* hold down the responsible position at the head of the reorganized industry that bore his own name. One felt impelled to almost any impossible task and to its accomplishment by the determined look of that lean jaw and by the knowledge of the powerful backing his approval and support provided.

"Where's Norine?" Scott asked irrelevantly.

Destinn flushed hotly. "I—I don't know," he stammered.

"What? She hasn't come to you?"

"No."

There was a curiously sheepish look about young Destinn. Chagrin, that was it. He was abashed that his companion's loyalty and concern seemed to be under question. A prey to sudden fierce emotion, Scott rushed into the library and called for a visiphone connection with Police Headquarters.

"Merkel," he snapped, when the face of the Chief stared out in astonishment from the disc, "I want the girl Norine at once."

"But Terris, you said not to molest her or—"

"Never mind what I said—get her! I want her at my place here inside of fifteen minutes, or there'll be hell to pay."

"Yes sir. As you say…"

Scott swore as he broke the connection. What in the devil was wrong with things anyway? Three weeks and more, it was now, since the girl had visited her stricken mate. What had happened at that time; had they quarreled? No, that couldn't be; she wouldn't desert a sick man, a man who had been part of her life—whom she had loved with all her intense nature. What then? His throat tightened in awful fear at the swift thought that harm might have come to her; she rose up before him in her vivid beauty, a vision to haunt him…memories came, which blasted and seared…

NORINE arrived, cool and collected, with two of the red guards. Scott felt the hot blood pounding at his temples as his eyes drank in her loveliness, and his heart leaped as his fears for her safety were dispelled.

"You sent for me?" she asked without emotion.

"Yes, Norine, it's Gail. He's well again—completely cured."

"No!" Her lips whispered the word and her eyes widened with a sudden glad light that brought in its wake a radiant smile and a flush of happiness. "Oh, Scott, where is he? I can't believe it. He—he can walk again? And use those strong capable hands—everything?"

"Yes, yes—come and see." Forgetting his own pain in her joy, Scott led her to the room where Gail and Arthur Mason waited unknowing.

"Norine!"

"Gail!"

The girl stood staring as the man advanced a step, stretching his hands toward her. Then she was across the room in a single bound, clinging to his fingers, laughing and sobbing in the same breath.

"Oh, Gail, Gail. I'm so glad—and so sorry."

"Sorry?" Destinn's eyes misted.

"Yes—about my last visit."

"Oh, that was nothing. You see, I knew the reason."

"Gail!"

Scott and Mason were tiptoeing to the door.

"Wait!" Destinn called out. "Wait, Scott. I think Norine owes you an explanation."

"No, no." The girl was pleading, obviously distraught.

"Yes." Gail was sternly insistent.

"All right then." Norine drew herself erect, flushing painfully as she faced Scott. "I'll explain. I'm not Gail's companion, nor the companion of any other man. I've never mated, legally or otherwise. I'm free as the air, Scott Terris, and intend to remain so. I made Gail tell you what he did because I hated those of the purple and was afraid; afraid of you and of myself. I've always hated those of the upper levels and their memory will forever remain a festering sore in my breast. The unsavory reputation of your men amongst the women of the sub-levels must have been known even to you, Scott. And there was my mother." She hesitated.

"Your mother?" Scott caught his breath. Angry, she was positively the most enticing...

"Yes, my mother. Twenty-five years ago a man who wore the purple broke her heart. The old, old story of a woman very much in love and a man who was too far above her station to marry. I am the natural child of this man. I don't know who he was, but I've hated him with every fiber of my being—I hate him now, and all his kind—"

"Norine!" Mason was advancing upon the girl, devouring her with eyes that held something of recognition, something of fear, and much of regret. "What was your mother's name, girl?"

"Rosov—I took it!" Norine stared wondering, her red lips trembling and her breast heaving with the stress of emotion.

"Norine Rosov!" Mason paled and his step faltered. "Norine! Great God, girl, I'm your father…"

"You!" The girl recoiled, then flung herself sobbing into the nearest chair.

Scott made his way swiftly and silently from the room.

HIS mind awhirl, Scott wandered through the laboratory and climbed to his old haunt on the rooftop. A cool sweet breeze from the river fanned his heated brow and the faint throb of the city's activity beneath lulled his turbulent senses as it always had done. He could think clearly here—and reason.

Arthur Mason's daughter! The thing was horrible to contemplate, in the thought of the wrecked life of the girl's mother and the undying hatred that had been implanted in Norine's heart. And yet, somehow, there had been an undertone of longing in her voice when she spoke so bitterly of the man who had loved and gone away; a hint of softening when the tremendous truth was brought home to her by Mason's admission. And Mason, he knew, was a changed man; he'd do everything in his power to make things up to the girl now. If only she would accept him.

And to think how she had fooled him about Gail and herself! In her hatred and mistrust of the men of the upper levels she had made Destinn a party to her little scheme, believing that Scott would not dare to take advantage in a situation of the kind that was pictured. And then he had taken that very advantage in a moment of madness and desire. No wonder she had turned from him in loathing and disgust...

They had quarreled about it too, she and Gail. Quite likely he had disapproved of her continued rebellion and had tried to argue her into a more charitable attitude. Good old Destinn; he had wanted to smooth things over and had failed.

It was no use. Norine was the high-spirited sort who would never unbend. She'd never forgive him for that moment of weakness—nor herself. With an infinite capacity for loving, she would steel herself against the possibility of again yielding to that power he knew had gripped her in that unforgettable moment in the laboratory.

And yet...

"Scott..." a soft voice whispered out of the shadows.

His heart missed a beat—two beats. Norine's fragrant nearness set it pounding madly once more.

"Oh Scott," she said hurriedly, and the white oval of her face looked up at him from its frame of golden hair made more glorious by the moonlight, "I couldn't hold out down there; there were two of them you know. And Arthur Mason is a wonderful man; he has driven all the bitterness away and—and things are different."

"Norine—you've forgiven him after all these years of hating?" Scott marveled. Anything might happen if this were true.

"Yes," in an agitated whisper. "And Scott, I want you to know about Gail. I've loved him—as a sister. But never...you must understand that I was afraid..."

"I know." Scott roused suddenly from his wondering daze.

She was in his arms then, miraculously, and the power of a great love swept down over them to carry them away from the world and from all thought of the past in its overwhelming might.

No words were spoken; none was necessary in that merging of two souls whom the vagaries of life had kept too long apart. Understanding came, and peace—the peace of that mighty yet tender passion that was to hold with them an undying force to the end of time.

Power! And love.

THE END

If you've enjoyed this book, you will not want to miss these terrific titles…

ARMCHAIR SCI-FI & HORROR DOUBLE NOVELS, $12.95 each

D-91   **THE TIME TRAP** by Henry Kuttner
          THE LUNAR LICHEN by Hal Clement

D-92   **SARGASSO OF LOST STARSHIPS** by Poul Anderson
          THE ICE QUEEN by Don Wilcox

D-93   **THE PRINCE OF SPACE** by Jack Williamson
          POWER by Harl Vincent

D-94   **PLANET OF NO RETURN** by Howard Browne
          THE ANNIHILATOR COMES by Ed Earl Repp

D-95   **THE SINISTER INVASION** by Edmond Hamilton
          OPERATION TERROR by Murray Leinster

D-96   **TRANSIENT** by Ward Moore
          THE WORLD-MOVER by George O. Smith

D-97   **FORTY DAYS HAS SEPTEMBER** by Milton Lesser
          THE DEVIL'S PLANET by David Wright O'Brien

D-98   **THE CYBERENE** by Rog Phillips
          BADGE OF INFAMY by Lester del Rey

D-99   **THE JUSTICE OF MARTIN BRAND** by Raymond A. Palmer
          BRING BACK MY BRAIN by Dwight V. Swain

D-100 **WIDE-OPEN PLANET** by L. Sprague de Camp
          AND THEN THE TOWN TOOK OFF by Richard Wilson

ARMCHAIR SCIENCE FICTION CLASSICS, $12.95 each

C-31   **THE GOLDEN GUARDSMEN**
          by S. J. Byrne

C-32   **ONE AGAINST THE MOON**
          by Donald A. Wollheim

C-33   **HIDDEN CITY**
          by Chester S. Geier

ARMCHAIR SCIENCE FICTION & HORROR GEMS SERIES, $12.95 each

G-9   **SCIENCE FICTION GEMS, Vol. Five**
          Clifford D. Simak and others

G-10   **HORROR GEMS, Vol. Five**
          E. Hoffman Price and others